TALES FROM THE REALMS: BEYOND THE WALL

Finish the Mission

Michael Weber & Brian Zeiler

Ten

16

For anyone who
has ever struggled
to find themselves.

Authors' Note

When we agreed to write this book together, we established a few ground rules to guide us:

1. We would take turns writing chapters.

2. Chapters would be 3-5 pages in length.

3. At the end of each chapter, we would write the protagonist into a corner.

4. We would complete the first draft of the story in one school year.

We stuck to those rules for the first draft, and we think it made for a fast-paced story. We'll leave it up to you to find where we bent the rules for the final draft now in your hands. So, sit back, grab your favorite beverage, and enjoy *Finish the Mission*.

Artist's Note

Readers with a keen eye will notice significant differences in the drawings for this book. There are several reasons for this. First, our idea of exactly what Na'lah looks like changed dramatically from the first draft of chapter one to the final draft of the book. As our understanding of her developed, so did the artwork. Second, my learning goals for the drawings also changed over the two years it took to write this book. Initially, I focused on studying foreshortening and creating finished products as quickly as possible. Later, my focus changed to improving picture composition and shading through the use of line proximity, cross-hatching, and line thickness. To aid my study, I used projected models (thank you, real-life Nahla, Khloe, and composite images from around Wisconsin!) to help me develop those aspects of my craft. Thank you for your patience as I grow as an artist.

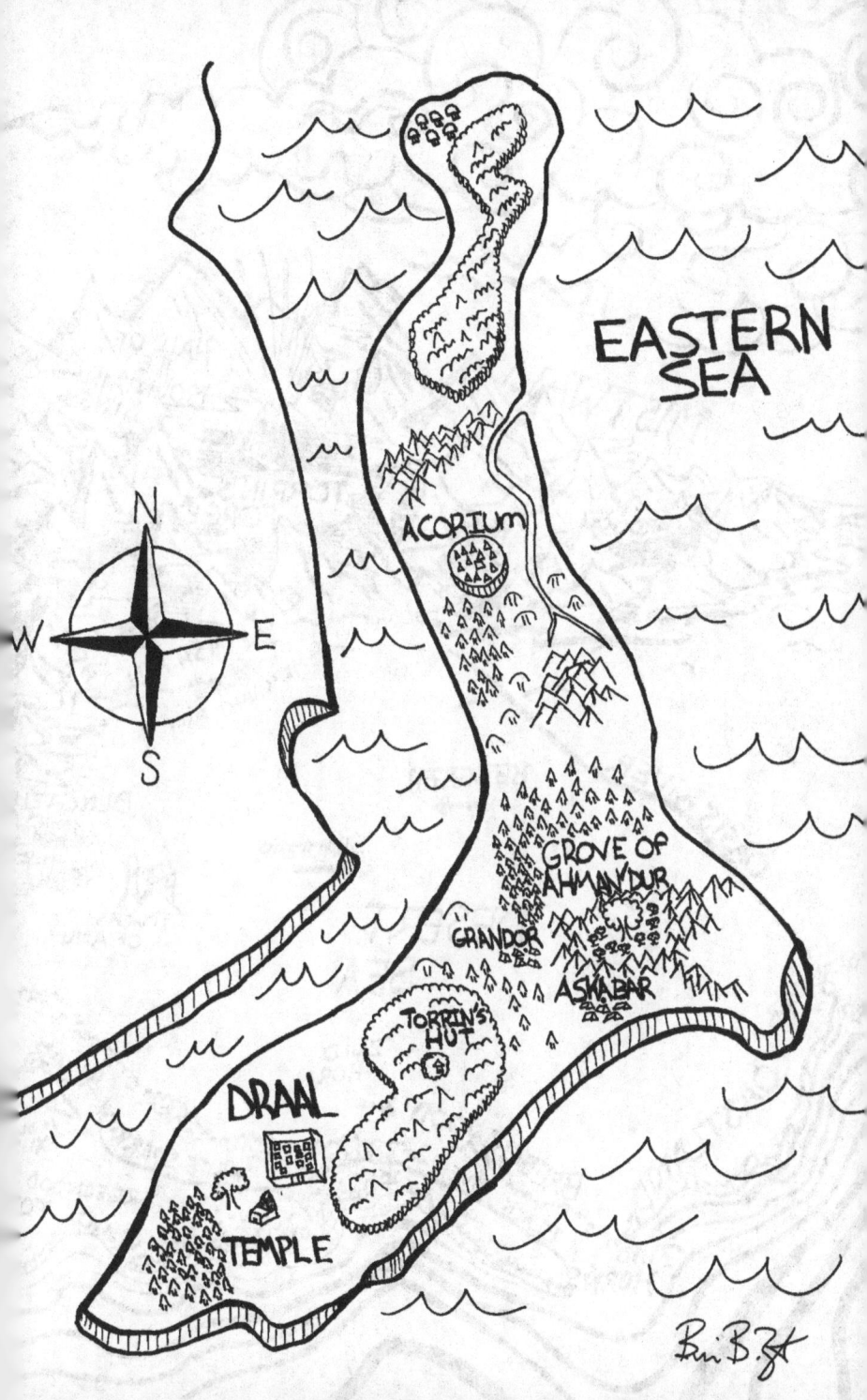

1

Your Brother's Keeper

It should have been an easy shot.

Na'lah, the forest goblin, crouched in a stand of white oaks, fifty yards above the elven village of Askabar. It was late afternoon. The heavy heat of the day settled on the valley like bathwater, making it hard for Na'lah to even draw a breath. There was cool to be found in the shade of the undergrowth, yes, but not nearly enough to keep the sweat from trickling into her eyes. *My blue eyes,* she thought, *the ones that make me different.*

"Take the shot," her brother hissed over her shoulder.

"Quiet."

"Shoot!" Badwin insisted.

Na'lah peered down the length of her arrow, past the body of her white ash short bow, past the cold, steel arrowhead, across the fifty yards of blistering summer afternoon heat, and onto the light, cotton shirt covering the exposed chest of her people's longtime foe– Alistar Elithium, the elven chieftain. Or leader. Or shaman. Or whatever. Na'lah and Badwin's contact had been vague on the point. His title didn't matter.

What mattered was that Alistar Elithium, a leader among the elves, was their target, and he was marked to die.

He was tall and lean, even for an elf. Nutbrown hair, cropped short in wood elven fashion, crowned a face with high cheekbones, a sharp jaw, and eyes so brown they were almost black. Na'lah rolled her head to the side to loosen the tightness in her neck. A vertebra popped in relief, and the tip of her arrow dipped.

"Shoot!" Badwin hissed. "What are you waiting for?"

Yes, what was she waiting for? One, well-placed arrow would ensure revenge for an elven attack on a goblin merchant caravan two weeks earlier. And elves and goblins had been killing one another for generations. What could be wrong with a little tit for tat? Na'lah snorted. What could be wrong, indeed? Na'lah was a hunter, an elite, in the goblin army. The best of the best. She knew how wars started.

They started like this.

So much for the recent ceasefire.

She shifted her shoulders beneath the leather armor she wore. Despite being sleeveless, the armor kept the heat wrapped about her chest and back. Dribbling sweat ran in rivulets over her shoulder blades, met in the neat crevasse of her spine, and rippled down, down, down. A trickle slid from under her leather cap, ran over her forehead, and plunged into the corner of her eye. She blinked against the salty burn and shifted her weight.

Badwin edged closer to Na'lah's ear. "Shoot!" he whispered. "They attacked a caravan!"

Above them, in the branches of an ancient white oak, three crows, as black as midnight, peered at Na'lah with shining eyes. *Watch! Watch!* they cawed.

Na'lah licked her dry lips and looked again. Below her, Alistar was kneeling next to a child. Askabar, an elven village of close to five hundred elves, was quiet this time of day. Most of its citizens found shelter from the heat in the deep shade of their porches, sipping on papuana juice, made that morning from the fruit of local trees, or dreaming lightly while caught in the clutches of a lazy afternoon nap.

But Alistar was not resting like the other elves. This afternoon, he took his time going from house to house, tree to tree, checking in with his people, catching up on concerns, and making connections. He knelt next to an elven child, who was showing Alistar a short wooden bow, the prized weapon of their people. Alistar smiled at the child, offered a word of encouragement, and then stood up and stretched, exposing the entirety of his unarmored torso. The child hugged Alistar's leg and then scampered off to join a group of children chatting in the shade of a nearby tree. Alistar, fists on hips, watched the child with a thoughtful smile.

"That's the shot. Take it!"

Na'lah ground her teeth. "I know."

"Then take it."

"I can't."

Badwin snorted. "What are you waiting for? He's a killer. All elves are killers."

But Na'lah was not so certain. There was something in her enemy's eyes as he knelt before the child. What was that? Kindness? How could the heart of someone who had killed so many of Na'lah's kin house anything other than anger?

Alistar turned and walked toward the center of the village. Badwin grabbed Na'lah by the skin of her upper arm, squeezing it so hard it pinched. He leaned in close enough for her to feel the heat of his breath, not to mention his frustration. The white of his teeth, fine and strong, flashed in the mottled sunlight. "We've been staking him out for three days, curse you. Take the shot. It's now or never!"

Watch! Watch! the crows cried.

Na'lah snorted. Her brother was right, of course. This was their mission. She drew the arrow back until the fletching scratched her cheek. The tendons of her strong forearms rippled like leather under her light gray skin.

Too light for a goblin.

Ghost Girl! Ghost Girl! came the taunts from her childhood.

4

Ghost Girl blinked against the memories. *Not now. Inhale.*

Alistar paused for a moment and waved at an ancient elf sitting on a stool next to his equally ancient wife.

Focus.

The old elf said something Na'lah couldn't hear, and his wife laughed. Alistar joined her. The sound of their cackling ran the length of the sheltered bay and echoed over the sleepy village. Fishing boats bobbed on the gentle sea.

Exhale.

"Do it," Badwin hissed, "or I swear to the Mother Tree..."

It was now or never. Na'lah set her jaw, set her eyes. A voice whispered from a cave deep within her mind. *He cares for children.* Na'lah shook her head, blinked against the resistance.

Across the courtyard, an elven woman dressed in a light green top and fitted pants, the common gear of elven rangers, stepped out of a building and waved to Alistar from the porch. "Alistar! There you are. We need you."

Watch! Watch!

Alistar returned the wave and strode across the courtyard. Beside her, Badwin growled. "Na'lah?"

He cares.

A flutter of leaves above them drew Na'lah's eyes upward. Two crows were tussling over a fish head, probably scrounged from the beach. The third watched Na'lah with unblinking eyes. Something in Na'lah's gut wriggled.

She blinked, and in that instant, the bowstring slipped through her fingers and twanged against the inside of her forearm.

The sharp sting of the bowstring slapped Na'lah's mind into clarity and caused the crows overhead to break into a chorus of cawing. The arrow zipped through the open space, its back end dragging slightly. Alistar whirled at the sound of the crows, turning just enough to catch the steel-tipped arrow high in his shoulder, rather than through the meat of his chest. He tumbled to the ground and rolled to safety behind a nearby cart.

"Blazing Sky Fires!" Badwin swore. "How could you miss that?"

Elven voices rose in cries of warning. The old couple on the porch shouted to elven rangers, who sprouted from doorways like mushrooms after a rain. The gnarled elf husband pointed up the hillside. "There they are! Goblin hunters!"

Na'lah dropped the bow to her side, her arms limp and heavy. The backs of her legs tingled and didn't want to move. She was the army's best archer. Why did she shoot? How did she miss?

Her brother grabbed her arm. "Na'lah! Come on! We have to move. Now!"

Everything felt thick and slow. Below her, more elven rangers rushed into the courtyard. Bows in hand, they scanned the hillside forest for goblin invaders. One of them, apparently catching the cue from the old couple, stabbed a finger toward Na'lah's hillside. "There they are!" The elf raised his bow and loosed an arrow. It zipped through the thick air straight towards Badwin's chest.

Na'lah's brother dropped to the ground, and the arrow slammed into the soft hillside next to him. "Great," Badwin grunted. "Just great." Badwin snatched up his bow and returned one arrow and then another. "Go!" he growled at Na'lah. "I'll cover you." He pointed down the deer trail they had used to creep deep into elven territory.

A chorus of twanging bowstrings announced the arrival of elven arrows. Slim ash shafts rained through the branches and leaves. One of these found Badwin's shoulder and punched through him so hard he spun around. "Blazing Sky Fire!" he cried. A splash of crimson poured down his sword arm. "What are you waiting for? Go!"

The sight of her brother's blood lifted the fog from Na'lah's mind in a flash. In an instant, she was Na'lah of the Short Bow again. Her eyes narrowed as she scanned the danger in the village below. Two more elven rangers popped out of a nearby hut, bows out, arrows at the ready. Na'lah raised her bow and yanked two arrows from her quiver. She fit the first arrow to the string with a well-practiced smoothness. *Inhale.* She drew the hemp bowstring to her strong cheekbone. *Exhale.* The first elf's movements were no more than flutters through breaks in the leaves.

That was all Na'lah of the Short Bow needed.

Release.

The arrow sprang between branches and into the village square. Sunlight flashed on fletching as the steel warhead thumped through an elven ranger's ribs. Na'lah's second arrow was on its way before the first elf crumpled, finding another archer's upper arm. The elf screamed and let her drawn arrow fly into the sky before dropping her bow and fleeing for cover.

Arrow after arrow leapt from Na'lah's bow and still the elves pressed forward. *How many of these damn rangers are there?* They fanned into a half circle, darting for cover to avoid Na'lah's deadly shafts. Step by step, the elven rangers tightened their net.

A rustle of leaves to her right won Na'lah's attention. She whirled in time to catch a fleet elven shadow slipping behind an old elm growing next to a knuckle of exposed granite. "I see them!" shouted an elven voice from behind the elm. "It's Na'lah! She's here!"

Curses erupted from the village, along with a few screams from the villagers.

"The Pale Demon!"

"The Ghost Girl!"

"Revenge! Revenge! Revenge!"

Na'lah smirked and refocused on the elf behind the elm. Raising her short bow, she took aim at the exposed granite behind the tree and let fly. The arrow streaked through the dappled light and shattered against the granite face. Splinters of ash and steel exploded in a swarm of shards. The elf behind the elm yelped and toppled into view, victim of Na'lah's makeshift shrapnel. He rolled on the ground, clutching the broken bits of arrow piercing his flesh, and groaned. Na'lah's next arrow found the elf's throat and silenced him forever.

More shouting now, as village guards moved into position. A quick count showed more than a dozen warriors on their way, in addition to the dozen rangers closing in on Na'lah and her bleeding brother. *What in the name of the Mother Tree did we stumble into?* Na'lah reached into her quiver for her next shot and her gut clenched. Only two arrows left. Not nearly enough. She glanced at Badwin's quiver. Even with his score of arrows, the elves would be on them in no time. Whether she was the Pale Demon or not, even Na'lah couldn't hold off a determined unit of elven rangers forever. Not if she wanted to keep her brother alive.

Slinging her bow over her shoulder, she lifted Badwin by his good arm and hauled him through the underbrush. "We gotta go," she grunted. "Now."

Badwin's face, normally a deep gray, faded to sickly green. The blood draining from his injured shoulder was thick and dark. Na'lah stopped to inspect the wound. Pulling aside his leather jerkin, she hissed at what she saw. The arrowhead was stuck halfway through his shoulder, making deep, grinding rotations in the meat with every step they took. Na'lah gnashed her teeth. Her brother was losing too much blood. If she didn't stop to bandage him right now, he would be dead before they came to the fork in the deer trail, just a short trot ahead. Na'lah lifted Badwin's arm from her shoulder and laid him on the hillside. Her brother looked at her, his eyes loose and bleary. "What are you doing? We have to run."

"You're bleeding out." Na'lah yanked a pouch from her side, where she kept her dried yarrow leaf. Grabbing a handful, she pulled the corner of his armor aside with her free hand. "Hold still. This is going to hurt." With nimble fingers, Na'lah packed the ground yarrow into the mangled flesh around her brother's arrow wound. Badwin hissed through gritted teeth. Then, without wasting another moment, she reached behind him and pushed the arrow completely through his shoulder. Badwin groaned. His head flopped to the right, and he vomited onto the hillside.

The blood came fast and thick. Na'lah moved with practiced precision, dipping her hand back into the yarrow pouch and packing more and more of the ground herb into the hole through her brother's shoulder. When she ran out of yarrow in her adventure pack, she raided Badwin's for more until her fingers clawed against the empty bottom of her brother's pouch. Badwin's head swooned. His eyes rolled back until only the whites were visible. His lids flickered once, and then he collapsed, unconscious, onto the hillside.

Na'lah shook his good shoulder. "Badwin. Badwin! We need to go!" She risked a look back down the trail.

The elves were at the base of the hill now, bows drawn, arrows nocked, creeping into the dense undergrowth. It was only a matter of time before the elves would be on them. "Badwin!" She shook him again, careful not to dislodge the yarrow packing.

It was no use. Her brother, his breath as weak as a spider's thread, would not respond.

The elves were halfway up the hill now, almost to the perch Na'lah and Badwin had used to scout the village. Once they found the goblins' trail, the elves would be on Na'lah and her brother in an instant. Na'lah grit her teeth. There was no way she could carry her brother to safety in his condition. He was simply too heavy for her to move quickly. If she wasn't careful, she could easily dislodge the yarrow packing, and he would bleed to death. With both Badwin and Na'lah's yarrow pouches empty, she would be powerless to stop it.

A shout from just down the hillside snapped her attention back into the moment. "I got a blood trail! Over here!"

Na'lah's stomach clenched. They were on her. It was only a matter of time now. She grabbed her brother's face in her hands. "Badwin. Badwin! Can you hear me?"

Badwin groaned. His eyes flickered lightly. Could he hear her? Crashes sounded up and down the hillsides. The elven rangers had picked up the trail. Na'lah scanned the shadows under the leaves, looking for the open spaces, hoping to catch a glimpse of movement while at the same time praying they wouldn't find her. "They're coming, Badwin. I can't carry you."

The rustle of branches and skittering of leaves announced the imminent arrival of the rangers. "Up here! More blood!"

"I want them alive!" a commanding voice called from the village. *Alistar?*

Na'lah's fingers dug into the side of Badwin's face. His skin tingled under her touch. "I have to leave, but I'll be back. They're not going to kill you. I promise."

More rustling. Closer now. "Two sets of prints! One's wounded. We've almost got them!"

Na'lah let go of her brother and crouched low. "I'm sorry," she whispered. She picked up her bow and let her last two arrows fly. Another pair of elves cried in pain.

The three crows took flight, offering Na'lah a parting piece of advice.

Run! Run! Run!

Na'lah watched the crows through the leafy canopy. Her stomach turned. How could she leave her brother? *Yet...* "I'm sorry," she whispered again. "I'm sorry!" With a final look at Badwin, Na'lah turned and sped down the deer trail to safety.

2

Returning Home
Empty Handed

Na'lah staggered the last fifty paces towards the North Gate of Draal, her head swimming. It was early morning, and the city was waking up.

How did it all go wrong? I never freeze. We scouted that shot for days. She quickened her pace. *I need new gear before I can get Badwin back.*

She nodded to the guards as she passed through the gates and then headed for the market that would take her to her dwelling. She looked to her right, where the Elders lived in their gated community. Goblin hunters stood guard at the gates, a job for third and fourth-year cadets. *Not fun,* Na'lah thought. *They live in their lavish dwellings, guarded, despite the walls around Draal, while the rest of us work to make their lives easier. Something has to change.*

Na'lah was so caught up in her head that she never saw Klier until she heard him.

"Na'lah! How did it go? You look like you were trampled by a horde of giants. Where is Badwin?" she heard from behind her.

She turned to find her childhood friend, Klier, in the mix of the crowd. He would have blended in if it weren't for his permanent smirk and waving hands. How someone could be that cheerful was beyond Na'lah. Especially after he left hunter training right before he graduated. What was he thinking? Na'lah put her head down, not wanting to make eye contact with him. She was in no mood to be cheery.

She stormed towards the Draal Market, which was filled with merchants selling their wares before the heat of noonday made it unbearable. In the past, the market flourished with exotic goods. But times had been tough, what with the war and all. Despite the meager offerings, the marketplace was busy, a gray tide that swayed back and forth. She chanced a quick glance behind her and saw Klier weaving like a bobber through the masses, trying to catch up to her.

"Na'lah, wait up!" he screamed, trying to get her attention.

She quickened her pace and dropped her head, determined to lose this fool of a goblin. She needed to keep moving if she wanted to get back to Badwin. But with the size of the crowd and the pushing and shoving of the masses, it was hard for her to get any distance from him.

Can he not get the hint that I don't want to talk? I need to get my gear and get out. She kept her pace brisk, wanting to reach home.

The back of her neck tingled. *Someone's watching me.* She glanced around the crowd and the market. Shoppers and merchants were gawking at her. That was nothing new. *Ghost Girl. Ghost Girl.* Then, something in the shadows of an alley caught her eye and darted back into the darkness before she could see what it was.

She dismissed it and, scanning left, studied the rainbow of awnings enticing the masses to buy fruits and vegetables. A hammer throw ahead of that, pickled meats hung from a string, absorbing the morning sun. A glance to her right showed the darker stalls of the market. These stalls were inhabited by people selling their wares and offering services. Any type of service, even if it was not allowed by the Council of Elders. Na'lah suspected the Council knew about the dark practices and took their cut of the earnings anyway. She snorted. What could a lone goblin do, anyway? Especially one that didn't fit in. A bit ahead of the merchants' stalls, white light and sparks danced off an anvil.

Na'lah froze as Klier burst through the crowd and headed straight for the blacksmith's shop. He snaked through the sea of people with the grace of a Shamanka, a temple dancer. A wheeled cart full of straw cut in front of him, and he slid under it, springing back up on the other side. He was a distance away from her when a group of kids playing "Whack the Elf" with wooden axes and sticks for bows stumbled into his path. Klier collided with them, falling face-first into the dirt street.

She hoped he might abandon the idea of catching up to her, but that hope faded as he picked himself up and resumed his pursuit. To Na'lah's surprise, Klier switched tactics and direction. Klier turned away from Na'lah and took off in a dead run towards the merchant stalls.

I have a bad feeling about this.

Klier headed straight towards the blacksmith's stall. He leapt upon the anvil, putting him higher than the crowd. He swayed back and forth to keep his balance.

"Na'lah!" he bellowed from his perch.

The market froze. All eyes turned to Klier, and then to Na'lah. She scowled, and the judging faces turned away. And just like snapping out of a daze, the pandemonium of the market began again, forgetting about the brief interruption to their daily lives. But that was when Klier finally made eye contact with Na'lah.

Na'lah mumbled a curse under her breath. *I do not have time for this.* She stormed over to Klier, elbowing the crowd to get to him. She yanked him down to the street. "What are you doing, you fool?"

"I just wanted to know how everything went. And where is Badwin?"

"Do you have to let the whole market know what you're doing?" she asked. "I need to keep moving, but since you won't leave, we can talk in private. Follow me, you idiot."

Na'lah led him to The Broken Axe tavern, where she found a table in the back near the fireplace. There were a few patrons in the establishment, but it was early enough in the day that they could find privacy.

"Na'lah, what is wrong with you?" Klier asked. "Why were you trying to avoid me? We grew up together. Why so serious?" he jested while trying to poke her in the side.

She whipped out her hand faster than a snake and caught his finger before he touched her ribs. She gripped it tight and growled. "Try that again, and you will lose this finger."

"Ow! Ow! Okay! I give up!" Klier tried to shake his finger free. "Geeze. What did I do?"

She released his finger and leaned back on her stool. "It's not that. I lost Badwin."

"What? How?"

"I had to make a decision that I thought I never would have to make, that's how."

"What do you mean? You have the most successful missions of all the hunters in Draal. Paired with your brother, you were unstoppable. Everyone says he is the anvil, and you are the hammer."

"This time the hammer broke when the anvil fell."

"I thought it was a simple scouting mission on the outskirts of the forest to keep eyes on an elven village.

You were just getting information. You have done that hundreds of times," Klier said. "What could go wrong? You go in, spy, and come back. How did you lose Badwin?"

Na'lah bent forward and got right in Klier's face. "It wasn't a simple scouting mission we were on. Badwin and I were deep into elven territory. Places we are not supposed to be." She turned her head side to side to make sure they were not being overheard. "We were given a mission to take out a target."

"I thought..."

"You thought wrong," Na'lah hissed. "We were on our own. No support, no rescue. No one knew except the Council member who gave us the mission. We were supposed to take out a high-profile target." Na'lah looked around the small tavern to make sure no wandering ears were listening.

"Alistar was out in the open yesterday," Na'lah continued. "We scouted for a few days before that. We were told by the High Council member to put an arrow through his heart. He gave us this honor because he said we were the best. And I failed." Na'lah put her head into her hands. "And because I failed, Badwin got shot."

"Badwin is dead?"

"Might as well be. When he got shot, the elves were tracking us down. He was bleeding out. I had to stop and pack the wound. He wouldn't make it," she stammered. "Klier, I had to leave him, or we both would have been captured or killed." She sounded as if she was pleading with Klier to absolve her from leaving her brother. "I had to go," she shouted, jumping out of her seat and grabbing his tunic.

All conversation in The Broken Axe stopped. Heads turned towards them.

A heartbeat passed, and Na'lah shoved Klier back down.

As soon as the vulnerability and sadness crossed her face, it was gone and replaced with the stone stare Na'lah was known for. Rage radiated within her, but she kept her body language calm. She was a lioness ready to pounce, ready to kill. "I have to go back for him. That's why I don't want any of your games. I need to resupply and go."

"Why not go to the Council member and tell him what happened? Wouldn't they send out a raiding party to retrieve your brother?"

"You don't understand. I was told it was a message to the elves to back off, but I fear that message was different. What I did was an act of war," Na'lah spat through gritted teeth.

They had been sitting there a while when the sun reached its highest point. More light flooded into the small tavern, illuminating the corners of the pub. Merchants and buyers were evacuating the market to avoid the midday heat. This time of year, the heat at its apex could make any hardened goblin's ears wilt past their shoulders. It was just unbearable to stand for long periods.

Inside, Na'lah squirmed in her seat. The light coming into the tavern was making its way to the corners of the establishment. Na'lah preferred to be in the shadows. She felt comfortable in the background or in the woods, in some shrub or bush. She was more alive outside this city than in it. She could not understand the pull of the market or city life for that matter. The bumping into people. The haggling over some small trinket or item needed. The tightness of the living quarters. The constant stares. She would have been happy living in a small hut outside Draal like her parents, but being a hunter demanded that she live within the walls.

A waitress came over to grab their order. Na'lah's scowl shooed her away. "I need to get out of this place, grab my gear, and go save Badwin," Na'lah whispered as she looked around the tavern. "I feel cramped, cornered like a caged animal." She turned from side to side, ready for an attacker that was not there.

"Na'lah, calm down. We're in Draal. You're safe. You are starting to sound like you believe in Spirit Walkers."

"I don't believe in foolish ghost stories."

"Go home and get some rest. You can't save Badwin like this. You've been out in the woods. You're exhausted. Sleep, and we will figure out what to do. You can't make decisions at this point," Klier told her. "I'll come and get you in a bit. Don't worry. We'll get Badwin back."

It would get her nowhere to argue with him. Klier was right, though. She was feeling haggard. "Fine. Come get me later."

Na'lah stepped out of the Broken Axe and into the blazing heat of the noonday sun. Most of the crowd swarming the streets earlier had dissipated. The heat didn't bother Na'lah. When she was in training, she was in it all day and still concentrated on her targets. *You become numb to the environment when you are stuck in it*, Na'lah thought as she headed toward her dwelling. *But then why haven't I become numb to all the stares I get in the market?*

It was a short walk across the city, and she was grateful for that. Her gaze spotted the Mother Tree just outside the market, towering over the buildings. The leafless tree was a husk of what it had been, according to the tales her mother told. Her mother was one of the highest level Shamankas, temple dancers who served as priestesses for the people. But no longer. The tree had none of its legendary green leaves shaking in the gentle wind. It had lost its imposing feature of protecting the city and its people like an umbrella in the rain. It was said to be the gateway for dead souls to move on. Now, it stood dormant.

Dormant or dead.

A sense of dread washed over her, and she shuddered.

Still, she had that same sense of being watched again... here out in the wide open. *Must be tired.* Now that Klier had mentioned rest, a wave of weariness crashed over her. The events of the past day would have crushed any ordinary goblin, and Na'lah was far from ordinary.

Crossing street after street, Na'lah still wrestled with the feeling that something was wrong. She waved the notion off. Maybe Klier was right. Considering what had happened and her weary state, maybe she *was* seeing Spirit Walkers... seeing shadows where there were none. She should know better than that.

As she walked to her door, she looked up and saw three crows perched atop her awning, glaring at her. It was a small, quaint dwelling, big enough to store a few things while she was in the forest. She chided herself for acting like a novice hunter as she reached for the handle. *It will be good to get some rest and clear my head. I will need it to come up with something to save Badwin.* She opened the door and walked over the threshold.

She shuddered.

Na'lah's senses and feelings were normally spot on. And if she had listened to them, her world would not have gone dark. But the moment Na'lah crossed the threshold, someone threw a burlap sack over her head, pain erupted, and her world went dark.

3

Counting Your Friends
On Your Fingers

She came to consciousness slowly. First, there was the muffled murmuring of someone, *someones* she corrected herself, talking quietly. Next, was the realization that whoever was near her was speaking Elvish. Her shoulders and arms ached. Her nose itched, and when she tried to scratch her face, she found her arms were tied behind her to what, a chair? When she tried to move her legs, she found them bound as well. Na'lah's tongue felt thick and dry. She tried to swallow, but didn't have enough spit in her mouth to manage even that simple task. She forced her eyes open. Her world was shaded, dimmed by the rough sack over her head. The back of her skull throbbed. Na'lah rolled her head to relieve the aching in her neck, but stopped with a yelp. A sharp sting from the back of her head told her all she needed to know; her scalp was bleeding, and now it was sticking to the sack.

"She's awake."

A boot scuffed on the wooden floor next to her. Was she still in her house? She tried to peer through the roughly woven sack, but all she could see were faint pinpoints of light.

"Light a lantern, but keep it low." The same voice again. Female. Certain. In command. Definitely elven, with that annoying, cat-like lilt.

There was a metallic creak of a lantern opening. Some movement. Finally, a warm, yellow glow filled the room, and then quickly died down to a low burn. The flickering lantern light was dim, but it flashed long enough to give Na'lah the information she needed. There were three silhouetted bodies between herself and the lantern. Elves, by their frames. If she included the someone in the shadows at her side, there were at least four someones in the room with her. She assumed it was a room anyway, with the wooden floor. Was this her house? As her head cleared, memories of what happened trickled back in. She had been with Klier at the Broken Axe, he said she needed to rest, she went home, and then someone jumped her.

Someones, she corrected herself again.

Her heart thumped. Elves in Draal? How did they get into the city? Worse, how did they know where she lived? Na'lah's hands trembled as the fear set in. Was

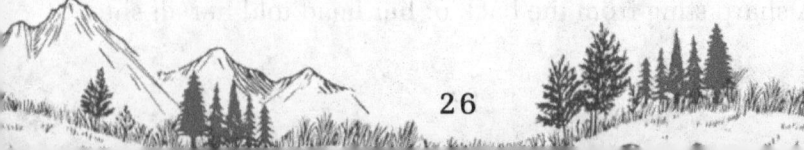

this an elven hunting party? If they knew about Alistar, she was as good as dead.

The shaking threatened to boil from her chest. If she was going to make it out of this, she needed to keep her wits about her. She licked her cracked lips. *Don't let them know you're afraid.*

Na'lah tried to speak, but the dust from the burlap sack gave her a coughing fit. When her throat was clear, she grunted. "Elves in Draal? You won't survive long."

Leather armor creaked as the someone standing by her side, the speaker, squatted next to Na'lah's chair. "Don't worry about us," the female elf said, her voice low and sure. "We got into your cesspool of a city easily enough. We can find our way out just as well." The elf shifted her weight, her boots scraping grit against a wooden floor. "You're pale for a goblin, aren't you, Na'lah? And what's with these ears? Not goblin ears, for sure. It must be difficult, standing out."

Ghost Girl! Ghost Girl!

Na'lah fought the quivering in her throat. "What do you want? You don't want me dead, or you would have taken care of it already."

"True enough."

"Well, out with it then, elven dog. I haven't got all day."

Her captor snatched the back of Na'lah's head, digging her nails into Na'lah's split scalp, and yanked her head back until Na'lah thought her neck was going to break. The elf pushed her face against Na'lah's ear and hissed. "Watch your tongue, assassin. You're not in a position to be cocky."

"I've been in worse."

The elf snorted. "We'll see about that." She tossed Na'lah's head forward, bouncing her head off her chest. The elf stood, leather armor creaking, and moved away. Her soft, elven boots whispered over the wooden plank floor. "Break her shooting finger."

"What?" Na'lah sat up straight. Her heart, a wild stallion, stampeded around and around her ribs.

One of the silhouettes strode quickly around the chair and crouched at her side. Na'lah balled her fingers into a tight fist, but the elf pried her right index finger away and bent it backwards until it snapped like a carrot. White pain flashed in Na'lah's eyes. Something roiled in her gut, and a bubble of vomit rose slowly in her throat. Na'lah grit her teeth. "That's my shooting hand."

The leader chuckled. "Yes, so sorry. More mouthiness out of you, and you'll lose it."

"What do you want?"

"That's better. Yes, we wouldn't be in this hovel if we didn't want something. You're going to help us."

Na'lah shook her head. "Why would I help an elf?"

The leader took a slow, purposeful breath. "You love your brother, don't you?"

Her brother? Badwin was alive! Hope flared, and then a memory rushed in, unbidden.

Na'lah's cheek still burned. Crouched under the plum tree in the modest family garden, she nursed the stinging reminder of Mother's fury. Noone slapped faster or harder than Mother, with her supple hands. She was the High Shamanka, after all, trained as a temple dancer with arms that writhed like ashen asps. In days past, it was said that dancers could awaken the Mother Tree with their movements, open its belly to the Halls of the Dead to usher the deceased through the Gray Mists and into the afterlife.

But no more.

The Mother Tree slept now, and in its slumber, the ceremonies grew farther and fewer between.

Maybe that's why Mother was so angry. Maybe that's why Mother was so insistent that Na'lah become a Shamanka, like her mother before her. "A hunter?" Mother asked with a snort. "You want to train as a hunter? Who brought this foolish notion into your head?"

When Na'lah couldn't answer, Mother answered for her. "Your path was chosen before you were born. Nature listens to you. It always has. You are to be a Shamanka, like me. Like my mother. It is our way."

"But the woods–"

Mother held up her hand. "This is not up for debate. You are my daughter, and you will do as you are told."

It was always this way with Mother. Her way or no way. Na'lah lifted her chin. "I'm not your daughter." She touched her slender ears that rose to the sky, rather than lying low and flat like other goblins. She held her arms and displayed her pale skin, too pale for the gray goblins. "I don't look like anything like you."

Mother's eyes went wide. Her chin trembled, the rumble before a storm. Then came the crack and thunder of Mother's palm across Na'lah's face. Her head reeled from the blow. "Enough! You have no idea what you are saying." Mother shook until her entire body trembled. She pointed a quivering finger at the door. "I can't stand the sound of your stupidity. Get out of my sight!"

Na'lah turned and fled to the closest thing she had to nature this deep in Draal—their family garden. It was a simple plot with a few fruit trees and vegetable beds, really all they could afford on Papa's military stipend and Mother's meager wages from her work at the temple. But it was theirs, and Na'lah loved it. She crept under the plum tree Papa had planted for her when she was born and touched her burning cheek.

"Well, that was something."

Na'lah jumped at the voice and looked up to find the younger of her two brothers, Badwin, lying in the plum tree's branches, munching on a plum. She checked over her shoulder to see if Mother had followed her into the garden. She hadn't. "What are you doing up there?"

"Same thing as you. Hiding from Mother." He looked at Na'lah's cheek. "You okay?"

"Yeah." Na'lah dropped her gaze to her hands. "No."

Badwin flipped his legs over the branch and dropped to squat next to Na'lah. He spit the plum pit into the yard and inspected her face. "You're not bleeding."

Na'lah touched her cheek. "No, it's not that."

"What is it, then?"

"I want to be a hunter, like Papa. Like Garak."

"Eww. Garak? He's so old, he's practically dead."

"He's our brother. He's not that much older than us."

"Still, he's so... grouchy all the time."

Na'lah shrugged. "Well, not like him in that way, but in the hunter way." She glanced over the garden wall, across Draal, to the sleeping Mother Tree with its bare branches reaching over the city. "Anything would be better than praying to a dead tree."

"Careful," Badwin said with a smile. "She's got ears like a hawk."

"What? That doesn't even make sense."

"Neither do you, you stupid warrok." He punched her playfully in the shoulder. "Tell you what, you want to be a hunter?"

"Yes."

"Well, let's go."

"Go where?"

"Out of the city. To the mountains."

"What? Without Papa?"

Badwin laughed. "Who needs that old goat? You and me can manage just fine."

Na'lah studied her brother's face. "Are you serious?"

"As serious as a raiding party." He tilted his head back toward their house. "Go pack a bag. We can be out of the city before the sun sets."

"But Mother–"

Badwin waved his hand. *"Doesn't matter. What matters is getting you into the woods. If you're going to be the greatest hunter Draal has ever seen, we have a lot of work to do."*

Na'lah hugged her brother. "Thanks, Badwin."

"For what?"

"For understanding."

Badwin laughed and hugged her back. "Anytime. Now get that bag, but don't let Mother see you."

"Well?" the female elf purred. "Do you love your brother or not?"

Na'lah swallowed against the tightening knot in her throat and nodded once.

"Good. Then listen well."

Na'lah dipped her chin.

The leader strolled leisurely in a long arc until she stood before Na'lah. "You tried to assassinate Alistar."

"It wasn't me."

A snort. "No use lying. We have your brother, and we know he doesn't spot for anyone but you."

"I'm telling the truth! It wasn't me!"

"Really?" Then, to the elf behind her. "Her shooting finger. Cut it off."

"What? No! I..."

Na'lah strained against the bonds binding her wrists, fought against the lashings tying her legs to the chair. It was no use. The elf behind Na'lah pried her broken finger from her fist with one hand and held it out, long and exposed. Then came the whisper of steel sliding from a leather sheath. And then pain. White, hot pain as Na'lah had never known. The blade carved through meat and bone, gristle and skin.

She screamed then, and the elf covered her mouth with his bloody, hot hand. He pressed the gritty gunny sack hard against her face until her lip split. Na'lah thrashed her head back and forth, trying to break free, needing to scream again, needing to warn the Council that elves were in Draal, but the futile struggling only won a laugh from the leader and the other elves. Fury burned hot in Na'lah's chest, filling her limbs with strength. She bit down on the elf's hand, bit through the burlap sack, and sank her strong teeth into the backside flesh of his fingers. He yelped, tore his hand away, and cuffed her hard against the side of her head. "Enough," came the leader's cool voice from a little ways away. "I think she's ready to listen."

Her head spun. Even through the gunny sack, Na'lah could taste blood from the elf's finger. Despite the threat to her brother, anger gripped her tongue and wagged it. "I'm going to kill you."

"Of course you are. As I was saying," the leader continued, "you tried to assassinate Alistar."

"Maybe."

"Impressive. A slow learner. Take the middle finger from her shooting hand."

Na'lah's gut clenched. "No! Wait!"

The elf behind her pried a second finger from Na'lah's fist. The knife whispered. The pain flashed. Just like that, Na'lah was missing a second finger on her shooting hand. Pulsing hot liquid gushed over her quivering fists and dripped into a pool behind her. The nausea came then. Na'lah vomited into the bag covering her head. She spit into the mess, trying to keep it from her mouth. "Gods, what is wrong with you?"

The leader sighed. "I want the truth here, Na'lah. Nothing but truth and understanding between us. So, I say again, you tried to assassinate Alistar Elithium, yes?"

Na'lah spit more bile into the bag. "Fine. Yes."

"See?" the leader said to the other elves. "I told you she could be reasonable." She stepped closer to Na'lah's chair. "Now, an assassination attempt on Alistar is no small thing. And this isn't your first time, Na'lah. How many of our people have your arrows killed?"

"I've lost count," she hissed, and it was true.

"That, I believe. You've been a thorn in our side for many years, Na'lah of the Short Bow. It's time for revenge."

Na'lah snorted. "Fine. Kill me and be done with it."

"Oh no. While that would be satisfying, that isn't our plan at all."

"You've got me and you've got Badwin. If you don't want to kill us, what do you want?"

The elf took a breath, a slow, nasally inhalation. "Your skills are legendary among your people. Your name is whispered in fear around our campfires."

Na'lah snorted. "Your point?"

"My point is you never miss."

"And?"

"You missed."

Na'lah bit the inside of her lip. "No, I didn't."

"But you did, assassin. Alistar is still alive."

Na'lah grunted. "More's the pity."

The leader chuckled. "Indeed. You missed. Why?"

"I... I don't know."

"Interesting. Strangely, I believe you. I don't know why I believe you, but I do."

Na'lah tried to clear the dust from her throat. Despite the missing fingers, the wild stallion in her chest was tame for the moment, its ears perked and curious. *Use the clarity. Press them.* "Why are you here?"

"You're going to do something for me."

"Really? What's that?"

"You're going to finish the mission."

"What?"

"You are going to assassinate Alistar Elithium."

"What? Why?"

"Does it matter? It was what you were sent to do. Do it."

"I don't understand."

"Do you need to?"

"Yes. It will start a war."

The elf snickered. "Does the hammer question the carpenter? Does the brush challenge the painter? You are a tool, assassin, nothing more."

"But—"

"But nothing. You're not in the position to ask questions. I thought the act of liberating your fingers would convince you this is not a game."

"Why would you want me to take out someone like Alistar?"

The leader sighed. "And here I thought we were getting along so much better." The elf came close then, bent near until her mouth was right against Na'lah's ear, pressing through the gunny sack. Na'lah tried to pull away, but the elf grabbed the side of Na'lah's head with fingers like steel daggers and held her close. "You, Na'lah of the Short Bow, are strong, but you can be broken. *I* can break you." She reached down and ground her thumb into the stumps of Na'lah's severed fingers. Bolts of searing pain flared until Na'lah's head swooned. The elf chuckled, then released her hold on Na'lah and moved away. "You were sent to assassinate Alistar."

"Yes."

"You are going to finish the mission, no questions asked."

Na'lah forced herself to sit up. A buzzing lightness swept through her head. She was losing too much blood. *Think straight. Think straight.* "I have to get permission from the Council of Elders. They'll never let me carry out a mission on my own."

"Permission from the Council? Since when did that matter? You didn't have permission from the Council when you took your shot at Alistar."

"How do you know that?"

Someone, one of the elves off to her right, chuckled. "Quiet," the leader said. And then to Na'lah, "We know more than you think. You were not authorized to take that shot on Alistar, but I'm telling you that you will finish what you started."

Na'lah took several slow breaths. "This doesn't feel right. What if I refuse?" Then, "No. You're up to something. Just kill me and be done with it."

"Ah, well, I was afraid you were going to say that." She paused for several breaths. "Gentlemen, gather your gear. We leave."

There was a shuffling in the dark room, as though the elves were snatching backpacks from the floor and drawing them over strong shoulders. Na'lah strained to listen. "What? That's it?"

"Apparently." This from the leader.

"Wait. What? You just cut off my fingers, ask me to kill Alistar, I say, 'No,' and you leave?"

"Well, we are done with you." A pause. "But not with your brother."

The stallion reared in Na'lah's chest. "Leave my brother out of this."

"Too late. We suspected threatening you wouldn't work. So, when we return to our village, we will begin the process of putting your brother to a slow, and shall I say, very painful death."

"No."

"And don't worry, we will let him know that when given the choice, you chose Alistar's life over his."

"That's what he would want."

"Of course, of course. But Na'lah, is that what *you* want?"

Na'lah chewed the inside of her cheek. The taste of bile covered her tongue, and she refused to answer.

A silence fell between them. Boots scuffed impatiently over the dusty floor. One of the elves let out a quiet breath. The leader cleared her throat. "What is your choice?"

What choice did she have? She needed time. Time to come up with a solution. Time to find a way out of this hideous trap. And most of all, she needed time to keep these elves from torturing and killing her brother. What choice did she have? "Fine. I'll do it. But I need a week."

"A week?" the elven leader scoffed.

"I need supplies, a new spotter, and scouting." She flexed her wounded fingers. "And I need to heal."

"Very well. You have one week to kill Alistar, or your brother dies."

A door behind Na'lah creaked open. "And don't forget, we have eyes on you, Na'lah. Always."

There was a shuffle of soft boots over wooden planks, the door closed, and then Na'lah was alone.

4

A Bit Ticked Off

Silence hung in the room. Na'lah cupped her mangled hand behind her. She needed to staunch her bleeding and get out of the bindings. She flexed, tightening the rope around her for a moment before it fell loose. When she had movement in her legs, she wrapped each foot around the front posts of the chair and curled her feet. Tightening her thighs, she snapped her legs inward and flicked her heels. Both legs on the chair collapsed inward, and she pitched toward the floor.

She fell, arms bound and rolled to the right and landed on her shoulder. She crashed with a thump. In the blink of an eye, the ropes around her chest fell to the ground. Na'lah jumped, whipped her bound hands around her feet, and snatched one of the broken posts. She flicked the post up and ripped the sack off her face. Then, she barrel rolled forward into a crouch.

All of this took Na'lah less than two breaths.

She scanned the room for her attackers but only found an empty dwelling staring back. The front door swung on its hinges, creaking open and closed. She sprinted to the street, hands still bound, hoping to get a glimpse of the people who had attacked her. But she found no elves, only merchants reemerging after the high noon heat had passed.

"Blazing Sky Fires," Na'lah cursed. *They timed their getaway perfectly.* She turned back to the kitchen.

She headed for the dried herbs hung over the counter. She grabbed some yarrow leaf, turmeric, garlic, and a knife to cut the bindings from her wrists. Once she was free, she grabbed a leather strip off the counter and jammed it in her mouth. Next, she ground all the ingredients into a pulp and spread it around her wounded fingers. Pain flashed like lightning through her whole body. She bit down on the leather in her mouth to stifle the scream. Once the pain subsided, she wrapped her hand with a cloth that allowed her remaining three fingers to be free.

"I need two working hands to take care of this situation," Na'lah mumbled. "I don't take kindly to being bullied in my city, let alone in my own house." She inspected her bandaging.

Next, Na'lah poured some water from a jug over her head to wash out her split scalp. She scrubbed lightly and ignored the sting as she inspected the wound. Probably needed stitches, but there was no time for that.

She put a spoonful of honey and ground yarrow into a bowl and mixed it well. Then, she dabbed the mixture into the split and pressed a bit of fresh mullein leaf over it all to keep it in place. *Not the best field dressing, but it will have to do for now.*

Satisfied, Na'lah grunted and stormed out of the kitchen.

She went to her bedroom and knelt before an iron chest tucked into a corner. She opened the lid and slid her hand down the left side, flicking a hidden switch to open the false compartment at the bottom. There, she pulled out her spare adventuring pack and slung it over her shoulder. Right as she turned to leave, there was a creak from the front porch. Again, instinct and training took over. She dropped into a low crouch, and her shortsword flashed into her hand.

She crept to the bedroom door and listened. *Whoever has come to finish the job is going to get skewered.* She controlled her breathing and opened her ears. There was a small squeak, like a baby mouse, just outside the bedroom door. Na'lah sprang into action. She had her shortsword's blade pressed against the attacker's throat faster than a blink.

"Na'lah... what the..." the visitor gasped, looking down at the blade.

"Klier! What are you doing here? I almost ran you through." Na'lah exhaled slowly and removed the blade from his neck.

"I, ah, came to check up on you. To see how you were doing," Klier said in a shaky voice. "But I can see that you must have gotten some... Na'lah, your hand! What happened?"

"I had some uninvited guests." Na'lah sheathed her shortsword and held up the hand missing two fingers. She stalked back towards the kitchen, shoving past Klier, who was still in the doorway.

"Are you alright? Besides the hand, of course," Klier asked, turning to follow her.

"I am fine. Just ticked off," answered Na'lah. She rummaged through the cabinet and pulled out a bottle. She held it in her good hand and used her teeth to pull the cork. She took a huge swig, belched, wiped her mouth on her tunic, and held the bottle out for Klier.

Klier grabbed the bottle and poured some into his mouth. He choked and almost spit out a mouthful of the drink. "By the Mother Tree, Na'lah. What is this wretched stuff?"

"Ground ginger, turmeric, and arnica. It helps dull the pain. And it gives you a jolt of energy."

Klier handed the bottle back. "So, what happened here?"

Na'lah took another long drink. "What happened here was I was attacked in my own blazing dwelling. I was tied up and lost two digits in the process," she said in a raised voice. "And to top that off... they disappeared in the crowd before I could get a solid look at them." She

passed the bottle over to Klier. "All I can say for certain is that it was elves who were here."

In the middle of a swig, Klier sprayed the contents of his mouth all over Na'lah.

"Elves? Here in Draal?"

Na'lah wiped the spray off her armor. "And let's add *that* to the wonderful day I am having."

"How do you know they were elves?" Klier asked, wiping his mouth on the back of his sleeve

"They had that stupid elven accent. But the way they overtook me in my own home, these vermin were rangers. They also disappeared into thin air right after I broke my bonds. They knew what they were doing and the time of day to do it. If I did not have to kill them for what they did, I might admire their tactics."

"What did they want?"

"That's the strange part. They wanted me to finish the job we set out for a few days ago. The Elves want me to kill Alistar. What in the name of the Mother Tree? Elves want me to kill one of their own? Normally, I would agree to this without any complaint, but this whole situation has me wondering. Why do the Elves want this... and why me?"

"Does it matter, Na'lah? You get to kill their leader... with their permission. What more do you need to think about?"

"Again, something is not right. When I said I didn't have permission from the Council, I heard a faint

chuckle in the background like they had someone on the inside."

"Na'lah, think about it. This is a chance to kill two birds with one arrow. You go and kill the leader, save your brother from the four elven rangers that invaded your home, kill them in the process, and come back a hero." He slapped Na'lah on the shoulder. "Listen, you need help with this. I'll prepare to be your spotter."

"Do I have to remind you that you never finished training, Klier?"

Klier turned from the door. "You know I can keep up just fine, Na'lah. I have been around you and your brothers long enough to prove that. I'm like your third brother."

He opened the door. "Come and grab me at my dwelling when you are ready to leave." And with that, Klier left.

Na'lah turned to the sink and rinsed the wounded finger stubs. After drying them carefully with a clean towel, she grabbed more of the pulp she made before. She bumped her finger stubs when she went for a pinch more of yarrow. A flash of pain shot through her body but quickly subsided. *Good, the tonic is working.* Yarrow. Turmeric. Ginger. Grind. Stir. Just like Master Goggins taught her. She could almost hear his gruff voice in her head. Grabbing the paste with her good hand, Na'lah winced as she spread a healthy dollop over her wounds. Then, she wrapped the paste with the fresh mullein leaf and applied a fresh bandage.

That taken care of, she filled her adventure pack with more yarrow leaf, bandages, and a flint and steel. Something in the back of her mind was pulling at her. *What's wrong?* She went through her whole conversation while she was captive in her mind. *What am I missing?* She finished packing and slung it over her shoulder. *Come on... think!* she repeated in her head as she walked to grab her bow.

Anger flared when her bandaged hand wrapped around the riser of the bow. *How the hell am I going to shoot again? I can't pull the string back!* She stalked towards the door.

With her good hand on the knob, she paused. Her bow clanked to the floor. Na'lah gave a blank stare at the back of the door. She opened her mouth, then quickly shut it. After a few moments, Na'lah growled to herself. "I never told Klier how many elves were in my house. How in the Mother Tree did he know there were four of them?"

5

Duck, Duck, Ghost

Na'lah slipped her arms through the straps of her adventure pack and then carefully pulled the mullein leaf bandage off her scalp. The knobs of her mangled fingers throbbed beneath the bandages and yarrow packing. She grimaced and tightened the lashings of her pack. With her good hand, the hunter grabbed her bow and stepped into the street outside her simple dwelling.

The sun was lower now. Na'lah held a hand up against the blinding light. *Late afternoon,* she guessed. *I must have been unconscious longer than I thought.* Na'lah took a breath to soothe her burning frustration. Hunted in her own dwelling. Her! A hunter! Humiliation heaped upon injury.

Na'lah growled and cast her gaze up and down the street. Merchants were out in force now that the sun was lower and the midday heat had blown away with the cool ocean breeze. There, a wiry fishmonger and his wife tugged a cart full of fileted salmon, smoked to golden perfection, into the shade of a mighty oak. A clam merchant, his stall already in place under the oak, threw his hands up in irritation. "Get your gray carcasses out of here! I was here first. Are you blind?"

Na'lah looked across the dusty street to find a pair of girls carrying light crosses of willow reeds woven into almond-shaped fans. "Beat the summer heat with our fans! Only two coppers!" One of them spotted Na'lah and waved. "Hunter! Hello! A fan for our city's top archer? Only one copper for our hero! A bargain!"

Na'lah grimaced at the reminder of her status. What would people say about Draal's top archer when they learned about her missing fingers? "Not today," she called, waving her good hand. "I've got places to get to."

And it was true. Badwin's life was on the line, yet she had no idea what to do next. On top of that, the reek of blood and vomit, not to mention the shame of being jumped, was too much to take. She needed to be outside, in the air, even if that meant the thick air of Draal's packed streets.

The road in front of Na'lah's quarters was fairly packed with merchants, their carts, and their wares. Several of them waved, but the hunter was in no mood for conversation. The elves had her brother, her long-time friend was acting suspiciously, and the elves wanted her to finish her mission to kill Alistar Elithium... so they cut off her shooting fingers? What in the name of the Mother Tree was going on? She needed answers, and she was running out of time.

A wave of nausea swept through Na'lah from her feet to the back of her blood-crusted scalp. She fought back the urge to vomit and rested a hand against her front stoop to catch her balance. *Think, Na'lah. Think!* Who could she turn to?

Maybe the better question was, who could she trust? Who could a hunter really trust anyway? There was her brother, Badwin, of course, but the elves had him. Her parents were not an option. And until just a few moments ago, she would have said Klier, but thanks to a foolish slip of his tongue, Na'lah wasn't sure she could trust him, either.

What about the Council of Elders?

Yes, the Council of Elders, indeed. How would they respond to learning that one of their members had sent Na'lah on a secret mission to take out an elven leader, in direct violation of the Council's orders?

"There has been enough provocation between our peoples," Elder Ontronus the Chinless had growled. *"We will not retaliate against the elves for the attack on Elder Narlak's wagon train. There is not enough proof that they were behind the atrocities."*

"What are you talking about? My workers' bodies were riddled with elven arrows!" Elder Narlak had protested.

"Enough!" came the reply. "We will not retaliate. Until we have more proof of their wrongdoing, we will not retaliate." Elder Ontronus the Chinless banged his wooden gavel. "It is decreed."

Elder Narlak had scowled, and as soon as the Council meeting was over, he summoned Na'lah and her brother to his chambers. "I have a mission that needs doing," he had whispered to them, after checking the doors and windows for interlopers. "And you're just the pair to do it. Time to show these elves they can't take advantage of us."

That was how Na'lah and Badwin had ended up outside the elven village of Askabar, with Na'lah's deadly arrow trained on Alistar Elithium's chest.

Na'lah's head swooned. Metallic saliva filled her mouth. She spit into the dust at her feet. Maybe Narlak could help her. Maybe he could point her in the right direction. But maybe she couldn't trust him either. It was all a gigantic mess.

Na'lah ground her teeth and steadied herself. The walk to the Hall of Elders normally wouldn't have been a problem, but with the blood she had lost, the dying heat of the day, and the questions swirling through her head, Na'lah wondered if she could make the trek without passing out. Taking a slow breath, she turned onto the street and pushed into the crowd, blending with the flow of traffic.

Weaving through the shoppers and vendors, Na'lah kept her grim visage trained just above people's heads to avoid meeting anyone's gaze. Not that anyone would have stopped a hunter in the street, especially one fresh from the trail, covered in dust and blood. But Na'lah didn't want to take any chances. She passed through the fish market, with its baskets of herring and cod, piles of nets, and fishermen, fishermen, fishermen everywhere, smoking their pipes, bragging about the haul that just got away, and popping corks from bottles of watered-down wine to ease the dryness of their parched throats.

From the fish market, she slipped through the shipyards and the warehouse district, where the sailors from other tribes gathered to swap stories and toss dice. A few of these sailors, perhaps emboldened by their bottles of watered-down wine, called out to Na'lah, offering to keep her company for the evening. On a normal day, she would have taken the opportunity to teach the cretins a lesson about proper manners, especially when addressing a hunter, but time was not on her side. She pressed on, past lines of taverns and the salty scent of grilled fish and potatoes. Her stomach growled. When was the last time she had eaten? Na'lah shook her head. No time for that now.

She was just passing a winemaker's shop when a shrill voice called from the alleyway between buildings. "Hunteress!"

Something about the voice caused Na'lah to stop dead in her tracks. She raised a hand against the late afternoon sun and peered into the dark alleyway. A shadow wavered there, cloaked and hooded. A single hand beckoned. "Come, child."

Rage flared in Na'lah's chest. Was that an elf? *No, too short. Or was it?* She snorted and gripped the hilt of the sword at her side. They wouldn't take her so easily this time. The figure beckoned again. "You seek answers, yes?" The air in the alley shimmered, like a mirage. A crow fluttered to an awning over the alley. Its black feathers shimmered in the sunlight.

A chill settled over Na'lah and gripped her bones. Her throat tightened into a knot. *Was* that an elf? It didn't sound like an elf. She cleared her throat and took a step toward the alley. She had to be sure. "What do you have for me, elf?"

"'Elf?' No, elf here, but come and see." The cloaked visitor backed away, fading into the shadows between buildings that were too deep for this time of day.

Na'lah shivered. Everything in her said this was a bad idea. Everything told her to run. This reeked of an ambush. *Go to the Council of Elders. Tell them what happened. Tell them about Narlak's plan. Come clean.*

But something else drove one foot in front of the other, and before she knew it, Na'lah of the Short Bow found herself stepping into the dark of a too-dark alley.

Na'lah squinted into the shadows, her eyes too used to the glaring Sky Fire overhead. She shook her head against the momentary blindness, and her head spun. From blood loss? From not eating since yesterday? The metallic stink of her own vomit tangled in her hair wafted on an alley breeze to her keen sense of smell. Na'lah went to rub her eyes and yelped at the sharp sting of bone fragments poking through the bandages. It was all she could do to keep from screaming.

She blinked hard against the sweat and blood, and the alley came into focus. Gray light streamed through the clouds overhead, casting thin rays into the dark alley. Wooden crates, brandishing the marks of foreign lands, packed both sides of the walkway. The bones of rotting fish, a shredded bed sheet, and a broken wine bottle littered the cobblestone. But directly ahead, where the struggling sun found no purchase, a shadow deeper than a cold well held court. Something moved in the shadow's depths.

Something old.

Something lethal.

Her tailbone tingled, and Na'lah gulped, fighting back the rising fear. "I'm here. What do you have for me?"

There was a sharp intake of breath, the rustle of tattered cloth over dry skin. "You are on trial, Hunteress."

A chill rippled the skin under Na'lah's leather armor. *Trial? Was this someone from the Council of Elders? Who ratted me out?* She took a breath to steady her nerves, fight down the trembling in her hamstrings screaming at her to *run! run! run!* "Trial? What have I done?"

"The spirit world is watching, Child of the Forest."

Na'lah swallowed, her throat suddenly dry. "And what do they see?" The thing rustled in the dark but said nothing. Na'lah gripped the hilt of the sword at her side. "Tell me."

Silence.

"Tell me!"

A wind kicked through the alley. Despite the blazing heat, a shiver seized Na'lah's spine and shook and shook until her teeth rattled. Then, came the voice, a whisper made of shadow, steel, dust, and death. "The spirits see a little girl who hides more than she hunts."

Na'lah scowled. "I'm a hunter. I hide from nothing!"

The shadow shifted, a cowled curtain drifting from side to side. *Was it getting taller?* Whatever it thought, it said nothing. Na'lah ground her teeth. "Me hiding?" She pointed at the figure with her mangled fingers. "Which of us is hiding in the shadows?"

A hiss wriggled on the breeze. Lethal. Warning. The cloaked thing crouched in the dirty alleyway, the worn robes settling about its thin frame with a puff of dust. "The spirits work best in the Gray Mist, hunteress, the space between this world and the next. We Walkers tread carefully there... as should you."

Walkers? Spirit Walkers? Na'lah shivered and took a step away. It couldn't be. Ghosts that walked between this life and the next? Ghosts that whispered to fortune tellers and prophets?

They were legends.

Not real.

Who would play at being a ghost? The trembling in her legs rose to her belly. She swallowed the urge to run and pressed on. "What else do the spirits see?"

"The lords of light and dark see a closed heart and a fixed mind. Crucial to your work up to this point, child, but in the coming trial, it will be the death of you."

"Death?"

"Lastly, your hand will bring the peace of justice to the land, but it will come at a great cost. Prepare yourself, child. The way will be long and lonely."

Despite the tremblings of fear, the lack of clarity made Na'lah's temper flare. She snorted. "What is this? Riddles and vague warnings? Give me something I can use rather than these stupid games!"

The elf, imposter, ghost, whatever it was, crouched in the shadows several strides from Na'lah and wriggled beneath its cloak, preparing to pounce. "Something you can use? Yes, there is something more the spirits have for you." The thing crawled on fingers and toes toward her; its thin fingers splayed like spiders in the dirt. "But are you strong enough to hear it?"

Na'lah swallowed and dropped into a crouch of her own. She reached for the serrated shortsword at her side, and in an instant, the cold steel was out before her. "Enough with the games. Speak!"

"Your arrogance has closed your ears to the spirit world's warnings. As a punishment, you will lose three things you thought you could not live without."

She held up her mangled hand. "Three things? Here are two already! Give me my third and be done with it."

The creature chuckled, a thin, wicked cackle. "So arrogant. A pity." It held up its hand, and Na'lah gasped when she saw it too was missing its shooting fingers. The thing lifted its hand to the cowl of its cloak and loosed a hiss.

Na'lah frowned. "What is this? A joke? Show your face, coward!"

The shadowed figure yanked back its hood and stepped into the light.

Na'lah's spine stiffened when she saw the face, her face, snarling back at her. "What devilry is this?" she gasped, knowing the truth of the matter now.

This was no elf before her.

This truly was a Spirit Walker, a guide for the dead, a nighttime story to frighten children.

Somehow, it was in the alley, alone, with Na'lah. She staggered back, arms flailing. Her breath came in quick pants, too fast to scream.

The thing wearing Na'lah's face swayed from side to side. Crouched on fingers and toes, it scurried at her like a spider. "Stay back!" Na'lah barked, brandishing her blade.

The thing gave a screech that froze Na'lah in her tracks. Before she could recover, it leapt at her and enveloped her in its dirty, tattered robes.

Na'lah grunted and fell back, slashing with her shortsword as she tumbled away. Robes rustled as the Spirit Walker crashed into her, covering her with dirty, coarse cloth. Na'lah yelped and slashed again and again. Her blade bit at the robes, should have met meat, but there was nothing there.

The crow perched overhead cawed.

Something behind her laughed. "Beware, huntress! Beware!"

Na'lah rolled away, freeing herself of the Spirit Walker's robes. Panting on all fours, she crouched in the alleyway.

A few steps away, the Spirit Walker's robes lay in a tousled heap. Whatever it was, goblin, elf, something worse, it was gone now. Na'lah took a few moments to catch her breath and then worked herself to her feet. White sparks flew before her eyes. "I need to eat," she muttered.

Slipping her shortsword into the sheath at her side, she stepped from the dark cold of the alley into the heat of the late afternoon sun. After her run-in with the Spirit Walker, she knew there was only one person who could help her untangle this mess.

6

Knock, Knock. Who's There? Master.

Na'lah was in a hurry to get answers, but her stomach demanded attention. She left the alley and turned toward the Draal market, where merchants sold various delicacies. Raw meats, fish, and fresh fruits hanging from the awnings were the people's favorites, but Na'lah was in a hurry. Passing stall after stall, she grabbed from writhing bowls of insects and flipped a copper to merchants without skipping a beat. If anyone tried to barter, the look on Na'lah's face shriveled them to dust.

She walked at a brisk pace, eating and throwing debris to the side. Crusted with blood and stinking like a barrel of rotten fish, Na'lah kept her hand on her shortsword. No one dared step in her way. Despite being in the market, her thoughts were still in the alley with

the Spirit Walker. *Death. Savior. Loss. What the Blazing Sun could all this mean?*

Na'lah shook her head. She hated riddles. Why couldn't things be clean and simple, like a good knife fight? She sighed and looked up. The sight directly before her staggered her back a step: a massive building of iron and stone, a rotten tooth rising over Draal.

The Iron Box.

What brought me this way?

It was the prison where the Council kept the most heinous criminals. A fortress of impenetrability. Seven floors high and cased with granite, the outer walls of the Iron Box were carved as smooth as still water. Small windows with thick iron bars were placed sporadically across its face to frustrate climbing. No one escaped. Ever.

Na'lah shivered under the blazing sun. She considered the Iron Box again. A guard posted before the ironbound front gate was sizing her up. *My looks cannot be encouraging here.* She glared back at the guard. "What are you looking at, Keeper of the Peace?" Na'lah spat.

"Let's not have any trouble here. Just go about your business, hunter." He tightened his grip on his glaive.

"If I wanted trouble, Keeper, there is nothing you could do," she snarled. He was innocent, of course, but at this point, her fury had to come out.

"Go on. Get out of here before I call more Keepers over." He pointed with his glaive to the side. "You hunters have no business here, not even you. Yes, I know who you are. Move on."

Na'lah looked at herself and grunted. She needed to clean up before she did anything else. She also needed to get away from this place. Too many bad memories haunted its shadowed windows. The memories of betrayal this place brought weighed heavily upon her. She spat at the guard's feet and walked away.

Na'lah headed towards the one place that felt like home: the hunter training grounds. It was a quick walk from the Iron Box. They had barracks she could use, now that she was not comfortable in her own dwelling. The training grounds offered her two things she desperately needed: a chance to clean up and someone to give her some guidance.

Spiked wooden palisades surrounded the encampment and reached into the sky. The posts were roped together and driven into the ground. There were no windows on the walls, but a large observation tower loomed over everything. The only entrance was a wide gate made of wood and iron that was always left ajar. Anyone foolish enough to cause trouble here would be dealt with by a horde of hunters-in-training.

When Na'lah reached the gate, her spirits lifted a touch, hearing metal colliding with metal and the grunts and pants of battle training. Two guards at the gate snapped to attention as she approached. "Hunter!"

Na'lah nodded but kept quiet. She walked through the gates and out to the courtyard, where instructors were drilling new initiates. The sounds of recruits training quieted. Heads turned.

"It's Na'lah."

"She's back."

"Just another mission for her."

"Master says she was the best pupil he ever taught."

Na'lah walked past the cadets and looked around. Sword training was directly in front of her, while to her right was hand-to-hand training. To the left was the archery range. Despite the day she was having, a small smile broke out over her face. This is where she grew up. This was home. Na'lah paused for a moment as a memory crept from the past.

Na'lah, a second-year cadet, stood at the shooting range. Her brother, Badwin, at her side.

"Come on, Na'lah. You can already outshoot anyone here, and you are just a second year," Badwin said. "Let's go train with the sword. At least I can get a few hits in on you. You never know when your bow will fail you."

Na'lah scoffed at that and nocked another arrow. "There might be an elf out there practicing harder. I need to be the best not just in here, but also out there. There are no second chances in the field," Na'lah answered. "Go beat up some of your fourth-year friends and leave me. All I need is the bow. And the bow never fails me."

She drew her string back and let the arrow loose. It thumped in the middle of the target.

"You never know when your bow might fail you."

"My bow will never fail me!"

"But what if you fail your bow?"

Na'lah tore her short sword from its sheath. "That's it! You're getting it now!"

Badwin yelped and scurried for the sword training grounds. "Not if you can't catch me, bow master!"

A voice snapped Na'lah back to the present. "Na'lah of the Short Bow. To what do we owe the honor of your presence?" A gray-haired, lanky goblin strode towards her, cane helping his limp as he walked.

Na'lah smirked. "Master Goggins. They still allow you to infect new recruits with your babble? I thought they would have gotten rid of you like yesterday's garbage. No wonder I haven't seen any new hunters in the ranks. You keep driving them off with your boring lessons on basics."

"I see those supposed talks did little good to a headstrong young goblin with piss and vinegar in her veins. That bratty little gray nuisance would listen to no one," he snarled as he engulfed Na'lah in a bone-crushing bear hug. "And I still graduate a few here and there. It is good to see you, Na'lah of the Short Bow. It has been far too long for this reunion, and by the looks of it, it has been far too long since the last time you washed off." Goggins pushed Na'lah back to arm's length. "What has happened to my prized pupil to come and see me in such a state?"

"I will answer all you need to know, Master Goggins, I promise, but first I must get the stink and betrayal off before I can clear my head." She gave a slow bow.

"Go girl, and once you have finished, you will tell an old master hunter your troubles, and we will see what we can do."

With that blessing, Na'lah was off to the barracks.

Night was setting in. Na'lah walked around the edge of the training field to a small, rundown cabin. It was tucked between two large oaks that branched over the shack, protecting it from sunlight and rain. The cabin could have been there since the beginning of time, with side planks hanging slightly off and its roof covered with moss and dirt. The door hung a little ajar and off-kilter. Na'lah headed for the cabin, now that she had a chance to clean up. Her bow was still slung across her back, and her shortsword hung loosely from a belt around her waist. She had grabbed a new tunic from a fifth-year cadet's supply chest without bothering to ask.

Na'lah knew better than to go through the front door. Instead, when she was fifty paces away, she got into a crouch and made her way around to the back. It seemed like even to this day, she had to prove herself to Master Goggins. There, she observed the cabin intently from a group of bushes where she used to spy on her master back when she was a cadet. The Sky Fire raced across the heavens, and finally Na'lah saw what she was waiting for. Between the small gaps in the sideboards, a light flickered off. Na'lah knew this was the moment to get closer.

Crouched, she edged through the brush. She peeled branch after branch out of her way and progressed forward. When she was ten paces from the house, she paused. *How to get the best of the old goat?* She took a small step to her right and readied her footing for the sprint.

Then, everything fell apart.

Her right foot sank a bit deeper than it should have, triggering a trap. Glass bottles rattled and clanked in a nearby tree. Instinct kicked in. She crouched lower, knowing the sound would alert anyone to her presence. But as she dropped, something tapped her left shoulder. She spun and had her blade out in a heartbeat.

"Na'lah... of the Short Bow. It seems your training has become lax since you left me. Come inside and tell me why I sense your mind is a thundercloud ready to explode," Master Goggins calmly stated, leaning on his cane. "And next time, use the front door."

Na'lah felt like a first-year cadet, sitting opposite Master Goggins at his table, ready for a scolding. Her left hand covered her right, hiding her missing fingers. Her face flushed with shame. "How did you find me? I took all the precautions."

"When the mind is clouded, all sense of creativity evaporates. Our minds tend to wander to the familiar for safety. You, Na'lah, were my most gifted student...creative, fearless, and loyal. You had a gift for the bow that I had never seen. It was an extension of your body. And your ability to disappear in any condition? Remarkable. If *that* Na'lah came to my cabin tonight, she would have been able to sneak in." Master Goggins paused and took a sip of his tea. He put the mug down and chuckled. "I have known you all your life, Na'lah. When you are burdened or frustrated, you go back to what has worked in the past. This old master still remembers where you hid the last time you snuck into his cabin so many years ago." Another small chuckle escaped. "I just waited for you there, knowing you would try again."

"I guess I am still learning, Master Goggins." Na'lah blew the steam from her mug.

"Ah, Na'lah, never stop learning because once you do, you will cease to grow. Now, tell me what troubles Draal's infamous hunter."

Na'lah recounted the whole story to Master Goggins, starting with the failed mission, the missed shot, and then Badwin's capture. She also told him that Narlak was the one who sent her.

"Hmm... Narlak you say?" Master Goggins mumbled while rubbing his chin.

She continued with the encounter in her house and told him of the elves that kept her captive. Reluctantly, she held up her hand to show him the missing fingers.

"My shooting fingers are gone, Master Goggins. I can still wield a sword, but how can I be a archer without the long shot?" Na'lah slammed her hand on the table and winced.

"Ahh, there's the famous temper. Na'lah, have I taught you nothing? Yes, fingers pull string, but that is not what shoots." Master Goggins leaned forward and tapped her forehead, hard. "Here is where you became a master of the bow." He tapped again. "And here is where you will master it again."

Na'lah began to speak, but Master Goggins cut her off. "Your story is upsetting, Na'lah, but it is not what creates the storm cloud in your mind."

She hesitated for a moment and shuddered. "I ran into what I think was a Spirit Walker by the market before I came here," Na'lah said in a quiet voice. "It told me that I will lose three things that I cannot live without. I have walked that thin line of Spirit Walker prophecy my whole life with my mother being a Shamanka, but Walkers are legends of the past. No one has seen one since the Mother Tree went dormant years ago, and even then, only Shamankas saw them. Or so they claim. Now one suddenly appears to me in an alley? Not only that, when it stepped into the light and pulled back its hood, my face was staring back at me! When I tried to grab it, it vanished! What magic is this? Are the old ways coming back to haunt me? Am I going crazy?" Na'lah shook her head. "Badwin is out there, and I need to go find him, but this Walker business has my head spinning."

Master Goggins studied Na'lah. "Na'lah, I know the ways of training hunters. But this, this is different. The

Spirit Walkers revealed themselves to the Shamankas, but only interacted with the Chosen, if legend is correct. You need to find answers before you can be whole again... and you know where your answers to those questions lie." Master Goggins paused. "Your family had connections with the temple, did they not?"

"No, no, they didn't! Those were all fake."

Master Goggins raised his eyebrows.

Na'lah coughed. "What?"

He sipped his tea.

"Just tell me!" Na'lah barked.

"The infamous temper. You will need to master that, Na'lah. I will not always be here to teach you." Master Goggins put down his tea. "To be whole again, you must reconcile your past. Someday, you will be sitting on this side of the table."

"What past?"

Master Goggins steepled his hands.

"Are you suggesting I need to speak with my other brother who has been locked in the Iron Box for the past three years?" Na'lah asked. "Sure, he saved me, but he is dead to me after what I saw. My mother and he are the reason they were exiled. I will never forgive them for that."

"Do you have to?"

"I don't know. You're my teacher. Do I?"

Master Goggins looked at Na'lah. "More tea?"

Your Brother's Keeper. No, Your Other Brother.

Night closed in.

Across Golden Bay, over the Eastern Sea where schooners rose and fell with the gentle tide, darkness unfurled from the horizon. Thin wisps of clouds, shredded sheets of white linen, stood out against the deepening purple. Moronia, goddess of the evening star, blinked herself awake and smiled upon the Realms. Soon, the fullness of night would cover the lands, and Moronia's kin would join her in their nightly dance across the sky.

Na'lah of the Short Bow slouched on her table at The Golden Touch, a funny name for a tavern known for its questionable stew and sour ale. Taking a deep quaff of the home brew, she studied Moronia over the rim of her mug. It was almost dark enough for what she had in mind. Her meeting with Goggins, her old mentor, had given her the insight she needed, but the withered hunter's advice hadn't been sitting well. Of all the people she needed to see, why did it have to be her oldest brother?

Na'lah scowled across the street at the Iron Box, Draal's great prison. Her eyes went to the sixth floor, where a lonely window looked upon the bay. Just the thought of her brother rotting in a prison cell brought a taste more sour than The Golden Touch's ale to her mouth. She took another swig to wash it away. Shame makes for a bitter meal, and her brother had provided more than a mouthful. The scandal. The prison time. The excommunication of their parents. What dark secret lurked around the next corner?

"Another ale?"

A waitress wearing a thin smock wiped the crumbs from Na'lah's table. Na'lah shook her head. "Just one tonight. There's work to be done." She fished a pair of coppers from her purse and flipped them on the table. "One for the ale and one for you."

The waitress snatched the clinking coins in a fluid motion and dropped them into a leather purse tucked into her belt. "Thank you, m'lady!"

Na'lah snorted and pushed back her stool. "I'm no lady," she said, strapping her bow over her shoulder. "Never was." She clenched her mangled shooting hand into a fist to hide her mutilated fingers. What would happen if word got out that Draal's best archer could no longer draw a bow? With a final nod to the waitress, Na'lah stepped into the evening.

Across Wharf Street, prison guards lit whale oil lanterns with flickering torches. Na'lah took a hard right and strolled southeast, away from the prison. The wharf along the bay was crowded this evening. Sailors from merchant ships stumbled in tight groups from tavern to tavern, jugs of burdock ale in their fists. Ladies of the night beckoned from the shadows, plying their wares according to the ancient tradition. There were few children to be seen, other than the rascals clinging to their mother's skirts as families hurried out of the inns and back to the quiet of their beds after an early evening meal. Things were just as Na'lah would have it, if she was going to break into the Iron Box.

A group of drunken sailors shuffled past, singing a shanty about a mermaid. One of them made a comment to Na'lah, but she deftly sidestepped the group and slipped to the bay-side of the street. There, she ducked behind a stack of boxes branded with the circular symbol of an anvil and hammer. "Zuid Horn," she muttered. "How goblins can live with humans and yakarii and," she spit on the wooden planks of the wharf, "elves is beyond me."

Sticking to the crates' shadows, Na'lah worked her way northwest, back toward the Iron Box. The famed prison loomed like a boxer's face against the last vestiges of the evening sky. Backlit by the stars, the Iron Box offered a dark silhouette with glaring black windows as eyes. Na'lah crept toward the prison until she was only one stack of chests away. Taking a breath to listen for patrolling guards, she eased an eye around the side of a container.

Three guards with long-shafted glaives paced the southeast side of the prison. "Meh," one of them muttered. "What rotten luck to draw the night shift again!"

"I'll say," another answered. "That makes three nights in a row. Angia almost tore my head off when I told her."

"She's mad at you for drawing the night shift?" This, from the third.

"Of course. What did your wife say?"

The third goblin guard laughed. "What could she say? I'm the master of my house."

"Sure, you are," laughed the second guard.

"You doubt me?"

"Maybe," suggested the second, "she's happy to have you out of the house."

"Why would she want me out of the house?"

The second goblin laughed and elbowed his fellow. "Well, that might explain why your son looks more like the butcher than he looks like you."

A round of curses darker than the coming night echoed over the Golden Bay. The guards continued their patrol and disappeared around the far corner.

This was her chance.

Na'lah sprinted towards the Iron Box. Calling upon years of training under Master Goggins, she leapt high upon the prison's walls. She hit the smooth wall lightly, wedging her booted toes and her remaining fingers into the scant cracks and crevices lining the prison's face. Na'lah winced against the white fire burning where her fingers had been. Gritting her teeth, the hunter climbed the prison wall, deftly skirting the windows floor by floor until she came to the sixth floor of the prison, where the most notorious traitors against the goblin clans were held. Even at this height, the wind couldn't dissipate the yellow reek of urine and the foul bite of intestinal waste draining from the prison's barred windows. Na'lah closed the back of her throat against the reek and crept to a blackened window she had stared at from the ground for the past three years. She eased herself closer to the window frame, and, after checking to make sure there were no guards below who might hear her, she chanced a whisper three years delayed. "Garak!" she whispered. "It's Na'lah."

Metal clinked in the prison cell. Something scraped across the floor, and then two stained hands with fingers like pale worms wrapped around the window's bars. "Na'lah," came a cracked voice. "Here to see me so soon? It's only been what, a brief three years? I wasn't expecting you for another decade at the earliest. How thoughtful of you."

Na'lah grit her teeth. "I should leave you to rot after what you did to Mother and Papa."

"Yes, well, rotting is what I've grown good at." The smacking of a tongue licking dry lips crackled in the silence. "If you came here looking for an apology, I'm afraid you'll be disappointed."

"You and Mother got Papa exiled."

Garak snorted. "There's more to the story, little sister, but you never let me explain."

The thump of boots below announced the arrival of a trio of guardsmen. Na'lah held her breath as they passed. The stumps of her mangled fingers burned. One of the scabs must have broken loose because the stones under her grip were growing slick with hot blood. Na'lah dug her good fingers into the cracks, and when the guards marched around the far corner, she continued. "Enough. I don't have time to rehash what happened. I'm here because I need information."

The pale fingers on the prison bars rolled and flexed in a practiced motion. "Information, you say? What could I possibly know that could help you? I've been locked up for three years."

"Don't play dumb with me, Garak. What do you know about Narlak the Elder?"

Her brother chuckled. "You got tangled up with Old Narlak?"

The muscles of Na'lah's chest tightened. Was her brother going to draw this out forever? "Knock it off, Garak. I don't have time for games."

"Why, dear sister, what happened? You must be pretty desperate if you're begging the black sheep of the family for help."

Na'lah took a deep breath and tried to release the tension and rising anger from her chest. "I messed up, Garak. I messed up bad."

Garak paused. "What happened?"

A knot rose in Na'lah of the Short Bow's throat. Behind the knot, the tension rose again, but this time it wasn't fueled by irritation for her brother, but rather shame. "I lost him, Garak. The elves have him."

"Who?"

"Badwin."

"Badwin? How?"

"The elves hit one of Narlak's caravans. Murdered all his workers. When the Council of Elders refused to declare war, something about there not being enough proof that the elves were behind it, Narlak had me and Badwin scout Askabar to see what we could find."

Garak grunted. "Sounds like Narlak."

"What do you mean?"

"I wouldn't trust him farther than I could throw him."

"What? Why not?"

Again, the march of boots sounded below, and Na'lah held her breath as another unsuspecting group passed by. "Enough!" her brother hissed. "Forget about Narlak. What happened to Badwin?" Garak pressed his face against the bars, and Na'lah gasped. His drawn face, so pale it almost glowed white in the fading light, was a shadow of the goblin he used to be. Dark spaces between his broken teeth winked behind cracked lips. "What have you done, you stupid girl?"

A jolt went through Na'lah, and suddenly she was a young goblinette again, cowering beneath the withering gaze of her eldest sibling. "It wasn't my fault," she muttered. "I had a shot at Alistar Elithium, and–"

"Alistar is dead?" Garak's eyes went wide.

Na'lah's gut swirled with the bitter brew of shame and regret. "No. I missed."

"What?"

"I missed."

"How?"

"I... I don't know."

Garak let out a breath and shook his head with a frown. "Na'lah of the Short Bow. Pride of the elite hunters." He snorted. "Even in your ignorance, you are a failure."

A legion of excuses rose to her lips. *The arrow hit a branch. My finger slipped. Another elf was blocking my shot.* But in her gut, she knew the truth. Na'lah of the Short Bow missed her shot at Alistar Elithium because she didn't know if she really wanted to kill him. But how could she tell her imprisoned brother the truth? How could he possibly understand? "I just... I'm sorry."

"Blazing Sky Fire. Shut up. Your whining is making me sick. No wonder you missed. How they ever let you in as a hunter is beyond me." Na'lah took a breath to respond, but Garak cut her off. "Don't bother with your stupid excuses. You still haven't told me what happened to Badwin. How did you mess that up?"

A flash of irritation seared the back of Na'lah's throat. By the gods, how her brother could drive a conversation! She shook her head and continued. "Their spotters saw us on the hillside, and one of their snipers got Badwin."

"Killed him?"

"No. Just a shot to the shoulder, but a bleeder. I tried packing the wound with yarrow leaf, but the clot kept blowing out. He would have died if I took him with me."

"A real hunter would have tried to get him out. Now we have a mess on our hands."

Na'lah's chest shivered with rage. "'*A real hunter?*' I don't think you understand what we are dealing with here. The elves are sending their best, elven rangers." She let go with her wounded hand and showed her brother the bloody stumps of her missing fingers. "The bastards jumped me in my own home. Look what they did to my shooting hand!"

Garak snorted and shook his pale face. "Blazing Sky Fire. What a failure."

An ember flared in Na'lah's chest. "Me? Who's in prison here? Whose stupid decisions got Papa exiled? You're the one that–"

Another group of guards appeared around the corner, and again, the conversation had to wait. Once the guards were gone, Garak shot a hand between the window's bars and snatched Na'lah by the collar of her leather armor. He yanked her toward him until she lost her hold on the wall. Garak grunted and hauled her up until she was dangling in front of him through the barred opening. A spear of ice pierced Na'lah's heart. She had forgotten how unnaturally strong her oldest brother was. Apparently, three years in prison had done little to sap it. Garak yanked Na'lah against the iron bars, still hot from the day's sun. He brought his mouth close so he could whisper with his sour breath into her ear. "Listen, you stupid *warrok*. You've stepped into something bigger than you can imagine. You think *I* brought a load of shame onto our family? You have no idea what you've just done."

"Garak! You don't understand! I tried–"

"Yeah, well, trying isn't enough, goblinette. You're playing with the big boys now. One wrong step could ruin everything."

Na'lah swallowed hard. The shame building in her chest was almost too much. Shame at losing her brother. Shame at losing her fingers. Shame at feeling like such a child at the hands of her imprisoned brother. As much as she hated it, hated him, she also needed her oldest brother like never before. And so, she swallowed both the lump in her throat and her pride. "What should I do?"

Garak's yellow eyes narrowed as he considered. "You have your adventure pack?"

Na'lah nodded.

"Give it to me."

Like a child obeying a parent, Na'lah struggled out of the pack. It wasn't an easy task, considering her mangled fingers and Garak's iron-like grip on her armor. But eventually, she worked the pack free and handed it to her brother. He kept her pinned to the bars with one hand and tossed Na'lah's pack into his darkened cell. Then, he studied Na'lah, still dangling over six stories in the air. "Grab the bars."

Na'lah swung herself back and forth until she could grab a bar. As soon as she had a grip, Garak let loose of her armor. "Meet me at Mom and Dad's tomorrow night."

"Wait! Mother and Papa's? What are you going to do?"

"You obviously can't save Badwin on your own. You need me."

"What? No! I just came here to see what you knew about Narlak and Alistar. Who is he? Why does Narlak want him dead?"

"Yeah, and look where that got you, *warrok*. I'm breaking out of this dump, and I'm bringing a few of my friends with me."

"No. Not–"

"*Him*, yes. Him too. The whole crew."

"Gods, no."

"Yes." Garak grinned at Na'lah, his broken, yellowed fangs glinting in the starlight. "But first, I've got to catch up with our dear parents. See you at home." And with a quick glance down, he shoved Na'lah from the window.

The last thing she heard as she fell six stories through the gathering gloom was her brother's cruel laughter, as cold as a knife.

8

Let's Have A Party

Startled, Na'lah awoke with a knife in hand, looking around like an ensnared animal. Everywhere she turned, complete darkness enveloped her, save for a shaft of moonlight pouring through an open square above her. She was lying in something wet, very wet, that reeked of rotting cabbage and eggs gone bad. After a quick dry heave off to the side, Na'lah noticed a cloud passing through the moonlight. The cloud strolled on its way, and the moonbeam turned into enough light for Na'lah to take in her surroundings.

What she saw made Na'lah gag. It seemed her beloved, incarcerated brother had dropped her through the wooden grate protecting the city from the foul septic system running beneath it. She was lying in waste from the Iron Box's more than two hundred inmates. Draal rarely rinsed this area of the sewers, knowing that years of stacked waste would deter any inmate from considering freedom.

"Great," Na'lah said. "Not only do I feel like crap, but now I am covered in it."

She clambered out of the cesspit and trudged shamefully back to the barracks to get clean.

Again.

She was getting sick of these delays. She needed to find Badwin.

Goblins parted before her, hands over their noses. Eyes darted away as soon as they saw who brought the stench. *At least they are not staring.*

"That's Na'lah, the hunter," she heard from the parting crowd.

"What is that stench?"

"She always was different."

She paid them no heed. Na'lah had more important things on her mind. She needed a new adventuring pack. Her old one was now being used to free one of the most hated goblins in Draal. Besides, she felt naked without the familiar pack on her back. She had gotten so accustomed to it, it felt like she was missing a limb, and she knew something about what that felt like. Na'lah made a fist with her mangled hand.

A short while later, after she washed off and grabbed new gear, Na'lah walked out of Draal and headed north. When her parents were exiled, they built a little farm near the elven and goblin border. It was deep in the woods and secluded from any traffic, but that was the way they liked it. Since they were banished, they wanted nothing to do with goblin society. Na'lah had not spoken to them since that day. She scouted their place many times, making sure they were okay, but she never interacted with them. Tonight would be different. Almost a complete family reunion. And she wasn't looking forward to it.

The mountain trail leading to her parents' cabin was hemmed on both sides with leggy stands of cedar. Young frogs hidden amongst the reeds of a muttering brook croaked in choral rounds. The scent of pine and running water danced on the warm breeze. Na'lah was a short march from the farm when she heard the murmuring of a low conversation off to her left. She dropped into a crouch, drew her bow, and scanned her surroundings. She crept towards the noise to investigate, slowing to listen. After a few moments, the pressure of holding the string became too great with her gnarled hand. She barely had time to unnock the arrow before the string slipped, dry firing the bow. Na'lah winced as the sharp slap stung her forearm and rang loudly in the quiet night. *By the Great Mother Tree, old habits are hard to break.* The murmuring she had heard stopped.

"Blazing Sky Fires," Na'lah cursed under her breath. She threw her bow aside and grabbed her shortsword.

"Who goes there?" an elven voice called out.

Na'lah went silent and still. *Elves? What are elves doing this close to my parents' farm?*

"I said... Who goes there?" the same elf said, but this time in a gruff voice.

After a few moments of silence, another voice spoke out. "Ehh... it is your imagination, Eldar. No one comes around here. Come, let's wrap this up. It reeks of goblins."

Na'lah counted to a hundred in her head as she was trained and added another hundred to be sure they were not still looking. She slowly sank to her belly and crept closer to the speakers.

She neared a clump of bushes and peered through. Four elves squatted around a small fire, talking with a fifth individual. The fifth was recessed into the shadows, head hidden beneath a hooded cloak. *Too short to be an elf.* She could not tell who or what it was, but tiny hairs on the back of her neck stood up. There was a familiarity to the fifth figure Na'lah could not place. She watched as the elves seemed to argue with the fifth person with frantic arm motions, but she was too far away to catch any of the discussion. Finally, the cloaked visitor raised his hands in a mock surrender, tossed a small leather purse at one of the elves' feet, and slipped into the darkness.

"Too dark to navigate goblin territory. We rest here tonight and head back tomorrow," one of the elves said. "Eat and bed-up. Tomorrow is a long hike, boys."

Na'lah knew better, but her curiosity got the best of her. What was in that purse? Not having the short bow to pick each one off from a distance made this a bit trickier. She would wait until they fell asleep to creep in and answer her question.

Night closed in as the campfire sputtered to a low glow. Nightbirds sang in the branches overhead and mingled with the steady rhythm of the elves' breathing. The moon rolled across the sky. Shadows from the looming cedars arced in black stripes over the underbrush. Finally, when she was sure all the elves were sound asleep, Na'lah slipped into the camp. She had seen them stash the leather purse in one of their packs. The moon was falling toward the mountains to the west, and the low campfire helped Na'lah stay hidden. When she was at the edge of the firelight, a loud screech like a crow being strangled rang in the night.

Na'lah froze. She sank lower, ready to spring into action.

"Mmmm... Eldar. Go back to sleep, you warg kisser," an elf muttered before rolling onto his side and falling back asleep.

"Kisser... kiss... her," mumbled Eldar, and he too rolled over with a smile on his face.

Na'lah was as stiff as a statue. She did not dare move or make a sound. She stayed prone for a few more moments before she crept towards the pack again. Sticking to the shadows, she was careful not to make a sound. Getting to the pack would take her out of the shadows briefly, but that was all she needed. She reached to lift the purse's leather flap...

"*SCHRIEK*," came the same sound as before, but louder.

"Eldar, I told you..." The leader rubbed his eyes with the backs of his hands and looked around. A spark from the dying fire shot sideways and reflected off Na'lah's drawn sword. The elf's eyes shot open. "What the... who the dungbar are you?" He stumbled to his feet. "Intruder!"

With one fluid motion, Na'lah hurled her sword and embedded it in the elf's throat. The elf looked down and tried to clasp the hilt. His eyes bulged. With a quiet gurgle, he toppled over and lay still.

Na'lah's was still in her crouch with her arm extended towards the dead elf's body when the other elves staggered to their feet. She loosened her grip on her sword and went for her bow, only to remember her critical mistake. She had tossed her bow away back in the brush!

Rookie mistake, she chided herself. *Going to have to do this the hard way, I guess.* Still in her crouch, she sank a bit more and propelled herself headfirst into the closest elf's legs. Something crunched as she bashed into the elf. She rolled to the side and sprang to her feet a few paces away. Na'lah spun and faced the remaining elves.

"What do we have here? A little goblin to play with," the elf on her left said. His eyes slid from Na'lah to the lump on the ground. "What have you done? You will pay for this with your life, goblin." The elf drew a thin longsword. He looked at the other elf and nodded, lunging for Na'lah together. The moment the elves twitched, Na'lah launched herself forward and twisted sideways into the gap between the two. The elves collided and stumbled apart.

Na'lah tucked and rolled through the gap. She came up with an arrow in her hand. *It won't kill them, but it will slow them down.* Na'lah flung the arrow at one of the elves' calves. With a satisfying thump, the arrowhead point buried itself in the elf's calf. He dropped to his knees with a grunt.

The other elf glanced at his fallen comrade and then made for Na'lah. He was quick. Normally, Na'lah's training would have made her quicker. But tonight, she was a touch sluggish. Na'lah sidestepped as the elf lunged. The elf missed, but so did Na'lah's planted foot. She tumbled to the ground, hitting hard. She rolled away quickly to create some distance and came to a crouched position near the bags. She eyed the remaining elves. One yanked the arrow tip from his leg and snapped the shaft in half. The other regained his balance and stared at Na'lah.

Time to end this little dance, Na'lah thought as she went through her plan in her head. *Dive, roll, elbow to the groin, shot to the throat. Sweep left leg of second elf and punch in...*

Na'lah's head slammed back and her body was slightly lifted up as a fist from behind found its mark. She found herself on the ground tasting blood in her mouth and seeing stars.

"Not so tough now, little goblin girl, are we?" The first elf was back, his eyes raging.

Stupid, stupid, stupid, Na'lah thought, struggling to find her feet. *Three, not two. Never lose track of your attackers.*

The elf that knocked her back came and stood over her. "You will pay for Lipin's life with yours, little goblin girl. What made you think you could steal from four elves and get away with it? You goblin hunters are all alike. You think you can just hide and... Umphh!!" He crumpled to the ground, holding his groin.

Na'lah rechambered her boot. She rolled to safety and sprang to her feet, pulling two more arrows from her quiver.

The elves grabbed their injured comrade by the belt. "Come on. We got what we came for. No need to stick around. Someone was bound to hear. Plus, we have to get that package back."

"What about Lipin?"

"He's dead. He was dead before he hit the ground. The purse is what we came for." Then, he kicked the ground and sent dirt at Na'lah's face.

Na'lah spun around, but a fraction too late. Some of the dust got in her eyes. She dropped the arrows and grabbed her canteen, splashing some water into her hand. It took only a moment to see again, but by the time she focused, the elves had grabbed their packs and were lost in the woods.

This day keeps getting better and better, Na'lah thought. *No time to chase. Garak will have my hide if I'm later than I already am.* She stooped, pulled her shortsword from Lipin's throat, and wiped the blade on his tunic. Resheathing her weapon, Na'lah checked after the elves one final time. Sure they weren't backtracking, she plunged into the woods the way she came. She was late. Too late, and she had to find the trail to her parents' cabin before the last of the moonlight was completely gone. It wouldn't be long now, and the family would be back together. "A family reunion," she whispered as the moon slipped behind the shoulder of the western mountains. "I can't wait."

Na'lah strolled up to her parents' hut a short while later. Garak slipped out of the woods, as silent as a dying breath. Several shapes lurked behind him in the shadows. *His gang... great.*

A branch cracked behind her. Na'lah spun and hurled her shortsword toward the sound. It slammed into the base of a tree and waved back and forth between a cloaked figure's legs.

The figure pulled its hood back. "Na'lah, be careful! Someone could get hurt!" Klier grabbed the hilt of the blade and pulled it free.

"Where did you come from, Klier?" Na'lah asked.

"I saw you leave Draal, so I followed you here."

"Then where were you when I was battling those elves back there?" Na'lah spat.

"Elves?" Garak asked. He looked to the woods. "Where?"

Na'lah shook her head. "I killed one and the other three ran off."

"Only one? Figures." Garak frowned. "The others are probably halfway to the border by now."

Na'lah tightened her grip on her bow. "We should go after them!"

"Easy, *Vengeance*," Garak said, strolling over to Klier. "Let's not kill Klier yet. We might need him to fix your mess." He gave Klier a glance. "Klier, take the crew and make camp by the old oak over there. Keep a low profile." He pointed towards the dense forest. "It is time Na'lah and I said hello to our beloved parents. It's been a few years, and we don't want to keep them waiting any longer, do we, Na'lah?"

9

Daddy's Favorite

The hut was modest by any standard. Crumbling wattle and daub walls struggled to support a roof of split cedar shingles. Thick fists of moss clung to the roof's ridges and trailed down the walls. A young plum tree, no more than a few years old, rustled in the light breeze. Garak fingered a bit of the emerald moss hanging from the eaves and frowned, the lines of his face like fishhooks tugging at damp cloth. "Blazing Sky Fires. What a dump," he growled. "Nice to see some things haven't changed."

Na'lah stood just behind her older brother, like she always did. How easy it was to slip into her old ways, tagging along at Garak's coattails, scavenging for a scrap of approval. "Knock," she said. "See if they're home."

Garak glared at her over his shoulder. "No kidding." He went to rap at the weathered planks and then

92

dropped his hand. "By the Mother Tree. Why the pretense?" He snorted and lifted the latch. "We're back."

Something shuffled in the dark interior, something hunched and bundled, despite the sweltering heat. "Garak?" came their mother's voice from the darkness. "Is that you?"

"Who else would it be?" Garak growled.

The figure stepped forward and placed a trembling hand on Garak's chest. "How?"

"I broke out of the Box. How do you think?"

"No. How did you know to come now?"

Garak stiffened. "What?"

"Na'lah didn't tell you? I thought she had heard."

Garak looked over his shoulder at Na'lah, his eyes dark, his frown deep. "Tell me what?"

Mother swallowed thickly. "Your father. He's dying."

Na'lah's heart dropped into the pit of her stomach. "Papa! No!" She pushed past Garak and rushed into the gloomy hut. The stringent bite of elixirs mixed with the ash of a simmering coal fire made Na'lah cough.

A withered hand, stronger than she might have expected, snatched Na'lah by the arm. Na'lah turned to find her mother's frowning face, more deeply etched than she remembered, but with eyes sharper than knives, scowling at her. "There you are, you wicked girl!"

Na'lah, despite years of training, despite surviving dozens of skirmishes with elves, despite being her people's most reliable hunter, shivered beneath her mother's steely glare. "Mother, I–"

"Silence, *warrok*. It's bad enough your father is dying. Seeing you might put him over the edge."

"I didn't know," she stuttered. "If I would have known, I would have come sooner."

The slap across Na'lah's face came hard and fast. "Lies," Mother hissed. "You've avoided us since *the Shaming*."

"No, Mother! You don't understand! I've been busy!"

"Too busy to visit the parents who bore the consequences of your blundering?" Mother paused and drew Na'lah close. The hunter, in her heart a quivering child again, was powerless against Mother's unusual strength. "Too busy... or too embarrassed?"

"I... I..."

Oddly, it was Garak who saved her. "Mother, enough. I'll deal with this *warrok* later. We've more pressing matters at hand."

Mother scowled. "More pressing than your father's passing?"

"Yes."

Mother turned her scowl upon Na'lah. "By the Mother Tree. What stupidity have you unleashed upon us now?"

Na'lah's mouth went dry. Her throat tangled in a knot. She flicked a dry tongue at her lips, to no avail. Mother's second slap flashed like lightning, bringing stars to Na'lah's eyes in the darkened hut. "Speak!" Mother screeched, her voice raising the roof. "Speak, damn you, or I'll flay you alive!"

Na'lah shuddered beneath her mother's fury. Her knees quaked, and a shiver took hold of her spine. "Bad... Badwin. The elves have Badwin!"

Mother shoved Na'lah away and whirled on Garak. "The elves have my son? Is it true?"

Garak shrugged. "So she says."

Mother turned toward the simmering coals, the dim light flickering in her desperate eyes. "How did this happen? Tell me everything." She turned her gaze, dark and brooding, upon Na'lah. "Tell me all, and pray I don't call the fury of the gods down upon you."

The words tumbled out of Na'lah then, a jumbled confession of excuses and apologies. The secret mission. The missed shot. The missing fingers. The questions. "We have to move quickly if we want to save Badwin, but there's so much we don't know. Why do the elves want me to kill Alistar? How is Elder Narlak involved? And how are elves getting into Draal so easily?"

Mother waved her hand, dismissing Na'lah's concerns. "Quiet, girl. I'm thinking. There are things at play that you do not understand."

"Na'lah."

The voice, thin and strained, came from the darkest corner of the dark hut. Na'lah peered into the corner, her keen night vision barely picking out a thin blanket over an ancient goblin lying on a dingy cot. "Na'lah, my daughter. Come see an old hunter before he passes."

Na'lah shuffled through the shadows, pretending to ignore her mother's glare, and knelt next to her father's cot. "Papa. I'm here."

The old goblin smelt of elixirs and ammonia, sheets that hadn't been cleaned in too long, and skin that hadn't seen the sun in months. "Where have you been?" He coughed and shivered.

"Papa. I'm a hunter. You know what I do."

"You could have visited, even once."

"Papa..."

"Just once."

A tightness gripped Na'lah's chest, and her mind raced back three years to the end of her training with Master Goggins.

Only three years ago, she was the star pupil, ready to follow in her older brothers' footsteps as master hunters. Both Garak and Badwin were honored members of the hunter ranks. Adding her parents' only daughter as a hunter would increase the status of their family's already substantial recognition. One week. Only one week, and her training would be complete. Only one week, and her official graduation would seal the deal for her family.

Then it all fell apart.

Na'lah had traveled back to Draal to visit the Mother Tree temple. Na'lah's mother was an elder Shamanka, one of the prophets chosen to care for the Mother Tree, one of the mighty trees revered by goblinkind, which allow the deceased to pass into the Halls of the Dead.

The Mother Tree had been sick for decades, dying, really, and the citizens of Draal feared that the gods had abandoned them. It was the job of the Shamanka to reassure the people that the Mother Tree was sleeping, not dead. If the people prayed hard enough, if they were faithful, the Mother Tree would awaken again.

Or so the Shamanka claimed.

While wandering the temple hallways looking for her mother, Na'lah stumbled upon a terrible scene—a room full of Elders and Shamanka around a low table covered with maps, pouches filled with coins, and bottles of wine. Among their number, Mother and Garak. Na'lah crept to the doorway and listened.

That was when she learned Draal's Mother Tree was not just sick.

It was dead.

And the Elders and the Shamanka knew it.

The words echoed round and round in Na'lah's heart, round and round, back and forth.

Dead.

Dead.

Dead.

The Elders laughed and drained cups of foreign wine, dribbles of red running over their chins, while the Shamankas looked on. Na'lah's stomach turned as she watched coins trade hands, listened to prophetic visions being written, and learned that the guiding of passing souls was not real. Not anymore, anyway. In fact, none of it had been real since the Mother Tree died. It was propaganda. A lie.

A tool to fool the masses.

A tool to keep the Elders in power.

Raised by a priestess, Na'lah's faith was woven deeply into the fabric of her being. Even though she chose to follow Papa's path rather than Mother's, Na'lah couldn't go into the mountains without tasting the divine. She couldn't look at the sun without feeling the warmth of nature's smile.

But now...

A cold, cruel chasm opened in Na'lah's chest. A cracked canyon that fell away at her feet until she tumbled into the vacant void, flailing, spinning, falling with no hope of ever touching ground.

Eternally alone.

Nausea washed over Na'lah. She tried to creep away. She really did. But everything felt slow and thick. She backed away from the door, but before she could escape, an iron grip seized her shoulder. "What do we have here? A little goblinette?"

Na'lah whirled to find Elder Moroni leering at her, his face close to hers, his breath cold and heavy, like old meat. She tried to jerk free. Moroni sneered and tightened his grip. "What are you doing down here?"

Na'lah gulped and shivered. "Nothing," she whispered, hoping the others in the room wouldn't hear. "I was just looking for my mother."

"Just looking, eh? And what did your 'just looking' find?"

"Nothing! I swear!"

Moroni's eyes narrowed to slits. "I don't think so. Your shivering tells me you've seen too much." He drew his dagger with a deadly hiss. "A pity. You would have made a good mate for someone." He brought the keen edge to her throat, ready to silence Na'lah and her knowledge of the temple's secrets forever.

That was when Garak arrived.

How he had known to come into the hallway, he never said. But before Moroni could strike, Garak's serrated blade was through the flesh of the Elder's lean neck. Na'lah stumbled away from the bleeding goblin while Garak rushed forward to catch the dying Elder's body before it crashed to the floor. "Go!" her brother whispered. "Or they'll kill you!"

And she ran. Through the darkened hallways. Away from the fear. Away from the shock of knowing the temple's terrible secret. Away from the corruption.

Away from her faith.

She escaped, but Garak didn't. He took the blame for killing Elder Moroni. It was his blade, after all, that did the dirty deed. When questioned about the murder, Garak concocted a story about a disagreement with Elder Moroni, who was known for his hot temper. What was not to believe? It wasn't the first time that goblins killed goblins in the halls of power, nor would it be the last.

But something had to be done.

An Elder was dead. Justice needed to be served and a secret kept. The trial was a public affair, with a convoluted story meant to appease the masses. Exile was the price Na'lah's parents paid to save Garak's life. He had killed one of the inner circle, after all, and there were some who called for his blood. But the inner circle protects its own, and the majority felt exile for the parents would be punishment enough. So, Mother and Papa were publicly driven from Draal, and Garak was sent to live out the rest of his life in the Iron Box.

And Na'lah?

Na'lah graduated from hunting school alone, save for her brother, Badwin, who stood where the rest of her family should have been had they not been exiled or imprisoned.

For three years, she had kept her secret. Not even Badwin knew what had really happened. He still thought Garak's temper was at fault. What would he say if he knew Na'lah's curiosity exposed the truth... that Mother and Garak were involved in a scheme to betray the city's faithful for a handful of coins? He would die of shame, Na'lah knew. It would kill him.

Just like it was killing Papa.

Na'lah knelt at the side of her father's cot. A trembling hand reached for her. "Na'lah?"

"I'm here, Papa."

"You should have come sooner."

"I know."

The scratch of leather shoes over the dirt floor announced Mother's arrival. "Torrin, let me get rid of the girl. You need to rest." Her voice, old and cracked though it was, carried the tinge of love Na'lah remembered from her younger days. As harsh as Mother could be, her love for Papa had always been real. "The girl brings death to our doorstep again, love."

Papa struggled to wave his hand. "Yes, yes. I heard." His bleary eyes searched for Na'lah in the dim light. "Daughter. Youngest child."

"Papa?"

"I heard your story. Listen." He coughed, the cords of phlegm thick in his throat. "My time is short, and, if what you say is true, so is Badwin's."

"I know, Papa. That's why–"

"Listen! You must be careful. Your mother and I, Garak, we all paid a price to protect you. And there are those who would see you dead. Garak knows. Listen to him!"

Na'lah looked at Garak, a silhouette framed by the thin light dribbling through the doorway. Despite three years in the Iron Box, a terrible strength emanated from her brother. A terrible strength and a terrible rage. She swallowed the thickness from her throat. "I will."

Papa coughed, and a series of convulsions seized him. Mother shoved Na'lah aside. "Out of my way, stupid girl. Can't you see he's suffering?" She grabbed a fistful of blankets from a dirty pile near the cot and stuffed them beneath Papa's back and neck to elevate him a bit. "There, love. Is that better? Can you breathe now?"

Papa hacked again and raised the thin blanket to wipe the corners of his cracked lips. "Thank you," he said, his voice scratchy, like sand on dry wood. "Na'lah, beware of Narlak. He seeks revenge. It was his brother that Garak's blade felled, and he has never forgiven our family."

"His brother?"

"Yes. He will stop at nothing to find revenge."

Na'lah chewed her lip. "Of course. It makes so much sense. Getting us to assassinate Alistar behind the Council's back would make Badwin and me look like traitors. If we had taken out Alistar and started a war, he could blame us and have revenge on our entire family." Na'lah shook her head. "I've been a fool."

Garak snorted. "That's nothing new."

"Quiet, boy," Papa said. Another round of coughing seized him. When he was finished, he wiped his mouth on a sheet.

Mother handed him a thin clay cup steaming with what smelled like mullein tea and honey. "Here you are, my love."

Papa took the cup and sipped at it. "Thank you, dear." Then, to Na'lah and Garak, he said, "My days are numbered, children. The water's in my lungs. Promise me this: that you will do everything you can to save your brother. Bring peace to our family, and you will bring peace to me."

Na'lah nodded. "Of course."

Papa cleared his throat, wincing from the effort. "Take care of one another."

"We will."

"And once your brother is safe..." Again, coughing, wheezing, and wiping of the mouth.

"Yes?"

Papa struggled to take a breath, the water in his lungs making his chest quiver. He reached out to Na'lah and pulled her close enough to whisper in her ear. She breathed in deep, and there, beneath the reek of ammonia and unwashed blankets, beneath the bitter foul stink of sickness, she smelled the scent of her father, who had once stood as tall and proud as an oak, a master hunter. She took in his scent and cherished it. "What do you need me to do, Papa?"

"Once your brother is safe," he whispered so only Na'lah could hear, "I need you to expose the corruption at the heart of the Council of Elders before they drag Draal into a war with the elves that we simply can't win."

Na'lah pulled away from her father. "Papa! No!"

He coughed. "Mother, Garak. Leave us."

Mother went stiff. "What? Leave you? You need me."

"I must speak to Na'lah. Alone."

Mother's lips pressed into a thin line. Her neck went stiff. Without looking at Na'lah, Mother rose with cracking knees and stormed out of the hut. Na'lah watched her go. Then her eyes fell upon Garak, who

snorted and shook his head. "Always Daddy's favorite." He left without another word.

"They're gone," she whispered.

"Good," he said. "There's something I need to give you."

"Give me?" Na'lah looked over her shoulder. They were alone. As much as she wanted to learn what he had to give her, a question burned within, a question that, perhaps, her father could answer. She took his thin hand in hers. Papa's skin was cool and dry, like parchment. "Papa, I have to ask you something."

Papa turned his rheumy eyes on his daughter. His breath rattled in his chest. He nodded.

"I saw something today, something I can't explain."

"Tell me."

"It was after the elves broke into my house, took my fingers." She held up her mangled hand. "In the market, just after noon."

"Go on."

Na'lah swallowed. *Blazing Sky Fire. I sound like a fool.* "Go on," Papa insisted.

She took a breath. "I was on my way to the training grounds when someone called from an alley. At first, I thought maybe it was an elf, coming to finish what they started. But this was no elf."

"What do you think it was?"

"You'll think I'm crazy."

"Tell me."

"It was, I think it was a Spirit Walker."

A whisper of a smile tugged at the corners of Papa's mouth. *Is he laughing at me?* Papa leaned toward Na'lah. "What makes you think it *wasn't* a Spirit Walker?"

Her spine stiffened. "They're not real, Papa. Ghosts aren't real."

The smile on Papa's face won out. His eyes closed. "Na'lah, we raised you better than that."

"You're saying ghosts are real?" Na'lah's chest trembled, not from fear, but from a simmering anger buried these past three years. "But the Elders! I heard them. It's all a lie! The rituals, the prayers, the will of the gods. I heard them. It's why you got exiled." The trembling reached her chin. "It's my fault. I never should have gone to the Mother Tree that day. Never should have listened. If I hadn't, none of that with Elder Moroni would have happened. You never would have gotten exiled."

Papa shrugged. "Maybe it was meant to happen."

"Oh, please, Papa. I'm not a goblinette anymore. I don't believe in ghost stories. I don't believe in prophecies, and I don't believe in the gods."

"That's the salve you've put over your wound."

Na'lah's whole body shook. "The Mother Tree has been dead since before I was born. The Mother Tree, the passage to the Halls of the Dead, the connection between this life and the next. It's all gone, Papa, if it ever even existed."

Papa's smile softened. He took her shaking hand in his. "You're angry."

"Of course, I'm angry! You and Mother were exiled for a lie!"

Papa shook his head softly and then changed tack. "What did this Spirit Walker say?"

The flaming coals in Na'lah's chest simmered. She shrugged. "It called me 'Child of the Forest.' Said I was on trial. Something about losing three things that are important to me." She snorted. "It doesn't matter. It's all garbage."

Papa patted Na'lah's wounded hand. "That remains to be seen. Some lessons must be earned."

"What's that supposed to mean?"

Papa took a slow breath and shook his head. "Time is short, daughter. You will learn what you need to learn. It's up to you to decide how difficult the lessons will be." He paused. "There's still something I need to give you."

Na'lah took her father's hand in both of hers. She knew when he was finished with a topic. No sense pressing him anymore. "What do you have for me?"

"Under my bed. My sword. Take it."

Na'lah reached under the cot and pulled out a battered scabbard for an ancient shortsword. "Isn't this your father's sword?"

"Not exactly," Papa said, his breath labored. "But now, it is yours. Use it well. Listen to it. You're the only one who can." And with that, Papa leaned back and closed his eyes. "Go, child, and let an old man die in peace, knowing that his favorite child will carry out his dying wish."

Na'lah held her father's sword before her and studied the cracked scabbard. There were so many questions. "Why won't you just tell me what I'm supposed to do?"

Papa reached for Na'lah, and she took his hand. "Because," Papa said, squeezing Na'lah's hand, "you are destined for greatness. But how to get there? That path must be chosen by you. Not me."

Na'lah stood and strapped her father's sword to her side. "You're not making this any easier." She bent and pressed her lips to her father's cool forehead. "I love you," she whispered.

Papa nodded. "Be safe, and send in your brother. There's something he needs to know." He closed his eyes and sank into his pillow.

"Yes, Papa."

Then, steeling herself, Na'lah turned on her heels and left.

10

Let The Good Times Roll

Na'lah left her parents' hut to find her mother huddled with Garak near the young plum tree. "Garak," Na'lah called. "Papa needs you."

"What does he want?"

Na'lah shrugged. "I don't know. He wants to tell you something, I think."

Garak grunted and walked over. "This should be good." He shoved the door open and went inside.

Na'lah pulled the door closed and turned to find Mother almost in her face. "Look what you've done. If you would have listened to me when you were younger, your father wouldn't be dying!"

"Mother, not now." Na'lah took a breath to calm herself. "Me being a hunter has nothing to do with Papa dying."

Na'lah's mother snorted. "Nothing to do with it? It has *everything* to do with it. You are my daughter. You were supposed to become a Shamanka, like me. That's what first-born daughters of Shamanka do. They follow their mother's footsteps so they can learn the ways. But you and your... your pride. If you would have become a Shamanka as you were born to be, we never would have been exiled." Mother glanced at the closed door. "And your father never would have gotten sick."

Na'lah growled in her chest. "You're still holding onto that? How could I live a lie, taking money from the Elders to make up stories?"

"Make up? Make up? Watch your tongue, *warrok*." Mother frowned and lifted her lined face. "Such a fool. You had the gift when you were a child. Your father and I saw it. The way the wind blew when you called. The way birds spoke to you."

Na'lah crossed her arms over her chest. "Coincidence and childish dreams."

"Dreams? You fool. You could have brought the faith, the *real* faith, back to our people. But when you started your training to become a hunter, your connection faded away. Gone!" Mother heaved a shaking breath. "And look where that has gotten us."

"'The real faith?'" Na'lah laughed. "I saw what I saw at the Temple. That's when I knew I couldn't follow a lie. I needed to follow an honorable path, unlike you."

Mother stiffened. "Watch your tongue, girl, before I tear it out of your mouth."

Na'lah snorted. "And you wonder why I haven't visited in three years."

Mother shook her head and looked at the mountains, rolling black shadows on the western horizon. "With a mouth like that, I'm surprised the gods haven't struck you down or sent a Spirit Walker to knock some sense into you."

Na'lah snorted. "Spirit Walkers? Were you listening to what I was saying to Papa?"

Mother's frown deepened. "What are you saying? Of course not."

"One of your Spirit Walkers came to me today. It spoke of nothing but dread and doom. I don't want any part of it."

"You... you saw a Spirit Walker?"

"Yes, and dismissed it like that." And she snapped her fingers.

Mother's face twisted into a snarl. "Arrogant as ever! Father is on his deathbed, Garak was locked up... and now Badwin is in the hands of the elves, all thanks to your stupidity," Mother spat at Na'lah, jabbing a condemning finger at her. "Yes, go. Ignore the warnings of the gods. Begone! You have done enough damage here." Mother shooed her away.

The door to the cabin opened. Garak stepped into the night. "What's going on?"

Mother waved her hand in Na'lah's direction. "Your sister is being a fool."

"Nothing new there." Garak looked at Na'lah and grunted. "Or maybe there is."

"What are you talking about?" Mother asked.

Garak shrugged. "Just something Father said. It was nothing."

"Nonsense," Mother said, waving her hand. "Go and retrieve your brother," she commanded Garak in a low voice.

"Of course."

"And Garak?"

"What?"

"If you are deep in elven territory, and you find anything that might help with the situation, bring it back. Let's see if that fixes the problem." She frowned at Na'lah. "This one surely won't."

"I'll do what I can," he said, and bowed his head.

Mother returned the nod ever so slightly.

Garak grabbed Na'lah's shoulder and led her back to the makeshift camp where the other hunters were waiting. He tapped their father's short sword, now strapped over Na'lah's side. "Nice toy, *warrok*. Daddy always liked you the best."

Na'lah spun on her brother. "What was that about?" She crossed her arms, her brows furrowed in accusation. "What does Mother want you to take care of?"

Garak pushed her again, and Na'lah stumbled. She cursed, but Garak didn't bother to look at her. "You worry about Badwin," her brother said, "and I will worry about Mother. You've messed up enough already."

"I'm not as inept as you think I am," Na'lah snarled.

"We'll see about that."

They entered a small clearing where the others were seated. Three figures squatted around a crackling fire, warming their hands.

Garak's gang.

Loyal to a fault, they went to the Iron Box for defending Garak when he was arrested three years earlier, after the incident with Elder Moroni. Master hunters all, they made a handsome dent in the ranks of the temple guard as they fought to save their leader.

Two of the figures were normal size, Klier and Skronk, but one was a few heads taller than the others. On seeing this figure, Na'lah rolled her eyes. She knew Garak was bringing Skronk, but it was still a surprise to see *him*.

Hobler.

Images of their past together flickered in her mind. The heat rose in her face.

Garak allowed Na'lah to take in the scene, and then he bent close to her ear. "What's the matter? I thought you would be more excited to see your old friends."

Na'lah bristled. She turned to the group around the fire and clenched her fists at her side. *Enough of Garak's games. I need to take control here.* She glowered at the crew around the low fire. "Listen up. The elves have Badwin, and he's wounded... badly. We'll have to move quickly if we want to save him. We're crossing the elven border before the sun comes up. We've got some reconnaissance to do before we can rescue Badwin. Here's the plan. Garak, you take Klier and him," she pointed a finger in Hobler's direction, "and scout the mountains west of Askabar," she commanded. "Skronk and I will take the eastern side. Badwin and I last saw Alistar in Askabar, an elven village northeast of the border, but he could have moved on from there. My sources say he takes the high sun months of the year to visit outlying villages. If we split up, we should be able to cover more of those villages. Badwin is a high-value target. Alistar wanted him alive, but that doesn't mean he'll keep Badwin alive once he's done questioning him. Time is short, so let's go!"

Na'lah bent down to grab her adventure pack. She slung it over her shoulder, making sure she could still reach the hilt of her father's sword. She did a quick test to see if the sword would come out of the scabbard freely. When she was sure, she addressed the group again. "Move out," she ordered, turning north, towards the forest. She was a few paces away when a crow squawked in the distance. She spun to find the group staring at her.

"What's wrong with you?" she barked. "We have to go. Now."

Garak crossed his arms over his chest. "Na'lah, no one is going anywhere. These men are under my command, not yours. We need a proper plan. Your arrogant lack of planning is the reason we are in this position. Get over here and sit down, little *warrok*."

Na'lah turned on her heels and glared at her brother. "Arrogant? Arrogant?" Rage tightened its grip on her throat.

Garak smirked. "Tamp the anger down there, *hunter*. I might have been imprisoned, but I still outrank you."

Fuming, she stormed back to the small campfire. She dropped onto a log near Skronk, who was flipping a dagger in his hand and catching it by the point.

"Long time no see, Na'lah. I'd like to say you've changed, but... ehh." Skronk shrugged and flipped his dagger again.

"Not now, Skronk. And knock it off with that dagger. You're going to get hurt."

"Old habits die hard." He flipped and caught the dagger again. "See?" he said with a grin.

Na'lah faced Klier and whipped out a finger. "And you. So willing to follow me out of Draal to save Badwin, but here you sit, wasting time. What's wrong with you?"

"I'm just here for the adventure."

Na'lah grunted and stared into the campfire.

"What? No hello for me?" Hobler asked, a grin on his face.

"You," Na'lah jabbed her finger in Hobler's chest. "You don't get to talk to me. Not now. Not ever. You made your choices, and they spoke loud and clear. So not a word from you while we are on this mission."

Na'lah turned to Garak. "Keep him under control, Garak. I don't want to deal with him."

Garak raised his hands. "Whatever you say... Na'lah." He addressed the rest of the group. "So now that our feelings are on the table, let's get down to business. After we officially checked out of the Iron Box, I reached out to some of my contacts. They told me Alistar will be in a western village by the ocean. We cannot confirm Badwin was with them, but he was traveling with a large caravan. Alistar, himself, travels with only a small group of personal guards on horseback. My contacts could not tell what the caravan was moving."

Skronk smiled, showing a row of sharp, white teeth. "So, we slip in at night, and I open a few wagons to see if they have Badwin." Skronk shoved his dagger forward and twisted it in the air.

"It won't be that easy," Garak replied. "My contacts also say the elven forest has been crawling with guards. They say the elven Elders have been searching for someone or something that has them on edge. The search has been focused on the southern part of their territory near the border." Garak looked around the fire and landed on Klier. "The elven Council is diverting all its resources to find whatever has them on edge."

Na'lah shot up from the log she had been sitting on. "So? We have dealt with elves before. We can deal with them now. We are all hunters here, save Klier. This is what we train for. So, let's do it."

"There you go again. Rushing in without seeing the whole picture, *warrok*." Garak shook his head. "The place is a tinderbox. Normally, we would move when they are not expecting something. But now, they are searching for whatever the Elders want."

"If we go in and get spotted, it won't be easy to fight our way out," Hobler pointed out.

"Exactly," replied Garak.

Na'lah turned to Garak like she wanted to strangle her brother. "We are wasting time discussing this! We have less than five days to save Badwin and to assassinate Alistar!"

Garak casually walked over to Na'lah and put his hand on her shoulder. "Let's just focus on getting Badwin back first. Going in there without a solid plan is a rookie mistake. As always, you're letting your emotions get in the way of your training."

Garak turned to the group. He paused and took a deep breath before he spoke. "Hobler, Skronk... I know you want to help me," he said looking both of them in the eyes, "but this time, I have to go off on my own. I need you to look out for Na'lah and Klier."

Na'lah whirled on him. "I do not need protection, Garak!" she spat. "I am a hunter, not your baby sister who doesn't know north from south."

"A fool and an imbecile is what you are." He towered over her, his face dark. "You see only what you want to see. And because of that, our brother is in trouble."

"And your eyes have been blinded by the Iron Box, or have you forgotten the last three years, dear brother?"

"I'm not as blind as you think, *warrok*," Garak responded through gritted teeth.

"Like at the temple? How blind were you then?"

"Sit!" Garak roared. After she was fully seated, he took a deep breath and composed himself. "Now," he said, "I need to take care of some business, but I have to do it alone. My contact is very... untrusting."

"Cap, we can come and have your back from afar. They would never see us," Skronk protested.

Hobler shuffled his feet and kicked at an imaginary stone. "Yea, Cap, I don't like this. Doesn't feel right."

Garak frowned and pointed at Skronk and Hobler. "You and you... with me. We need to talk." He turned and strode away from the fire.

Skronk and Hobler got up to follow their captain, leaving Na'lah with Klier.

Na'lah turned to Klier, her doubts about him still swimming in her mind. "You've been quiet. Why is that, Klier?" She studied him, trying to read his mind.

"Like I told you before, Na'lah. I want to rescue Badwin. He is my friend too, you know. But you left Draal without me, so I followed you in case you needed help. I didn't know about Garak and his crew breaking out of the Iron Box. I thought you were going solo."

Na'lah's temper rose again. "Interesting how you always show up at just the right time and place. And then when a fight happens, you are nowhere to be seen... or were you, Klier?"

Klier's eyes opened wide for a moment. "What are you talking about? I just came to..."

That's when Garak returned with Skronk and Hobler in tow. His presence shut Klier up. Both Na'lah and Klier turned to him.

"Here is what is going to happen. I am going to meet my contact. Skronk and Klier, you are going north and then cutting west towards the ocean. Hobler and Na'lah will head east and follow the coastline north."

Na'lah sprang off the log. "I am not going with that oaf of a goblin. I would rather have my other fingers cut off than go with him."

Garak turned on her, brows furrowed. "You can, and you will. Conversation done. Now, it's the BOX method we all know from training. It is the quickest way to scout the territory. Teams of two will be harder for the elves to spot. Focus on the perimeter. We'll meet up on the other side. When you find Badwin, camp, but don't make a move on him. Wait for everyone to arrive so we can make a coordinated attack. We will only get one shot at this. I will be back shortly and follow the route until I run into you."

Na'lah, still standing, clenched her hands tight. "I don't think..."

Garak turned to face her. "Agreed, you don't. Plan made. Done." And with that, Garak headed into the forest.

One by one, each of the members of the crew grabbed their packs and followed Garak, all except Na'lah, who stood with her mouth gaping wide open like a fish.

Silence settled over the campfire. A moment passed, and then a crow squawked in the distance.

11

Harken The Call

Bit by bit, morning's fingers tugged back the last traces of night, thin threads of black that faded to gray. Bird calls echoed across the mountainside as the Sky Fire crept closer and closer to making its appearance for the day. Below, in the shadows of the valley, a ribbon of river murmured to itself.

Na'lah was exhausted. She and Hobler had traveled east the entire night, using darkness to hide their passage deep into elven territory. They took turns leading, sharing the risk of running point. When she led, Na'lah's skin tingled, imagining Hobler's eyes on her. After three years in the Iron Box, Hobler had undoubtedly built up an appetite for more than just freedom, hadn't he? She certainly missed *him*. However, whenever she shot a look over her shoulder at Hobler, she found his focus on the mountainsides, scanning, scanning, scanning as he always used to when they ran missions together. Was she imagining his desire for her?

And when it was Hobler's turn to run point, Na'lah found it difficult not to admire the well-formed limbs of this hunter who at one time had been much more than just her brother's friend. More than once, Hobler turned and caught Na'lah's eyes upon him. Her cheeks flamed. By the Mother Tree! Why did everything have to be so difficult?

But with the morning came time to rest. They would have to move more slowly in the daylight, and they would do so after a short break. Na'lah, now in the lead, found a dense patch of black oaks clinging to the mountain side. *There*, she signaled Hobler, who lifted his chin in agreement.

They slipped over an exposed face of granite, still cool from the night, and settled down among the thick roots of the ancient oaks. Na'lah dropped her pack from her shoulders, wincing at the stabbing pain of her mangled fingers. She squatted against the oak's rough trunk and dug in her pack for a shred of dried venison. "Have some of mine," Hobler grunted and tossed a strip of jerky her way.

Na'lah looked up in time to make a swipe at the venison mid-flight. Quick as a cat, Na'lah pawed at the dried meat and would have caught it, save for her missing fingers. The jerky flipped onto the musty leaf bed. She snatched it up and chewed angrily, glaring into the thinning shadows beneath a nearby bush. "Thanks," she managed between chews.

"Of course." Then, "Sorry about your fingers."

Na'lah snapped her eyes back to Hobler, expecting to see the mocking glint of a smirk lighting his gaze. Instead, she found the soft eyes of concern, not unlike the eyes she had fallen for only a few years before. She cleared her throat. "Yeah. Thanks."

"They took your shooting fingers, cruel bastards."

"Tell me about it." Na'lah's chest tightened, not sure where he was going with this.

Hobler watched her chew, his gaze moving between her eyes and her mouth. "I missed you."

Na'lah snorted. "Really? We're going to have this conversation now?"

Hobler shrugged his muscled shoulders. "Why not?"

"We have a mission to focus on."

"Doesn't mean we can't talk." He stood and stretched like a panther, revealing a trim waist beneath his leather armor. Hobler came and stood next to her. "Mind if I sit?"

Something warm flushed in Na'lah's chest, and her throat went a little dry. She moved over a bit and jerked a thumb at the leaf bed next to her. "Help yourself."

He plopped down and moved over so their shoulders touched. A breeze whispered through the undergrowth, bringing with it the scent of Hobler's well-oiled leather armor, the sweat of a night's run, and something deeper that made her nostrils flare. "You know," he said, "this

doesn't have to be awkward. Just because of, you know, our past."

Na'lah snorted. "Our past? Need I remind you that you're the one who ended our relationship, not once, but twice?"

Hobler sighed. "I've had three years in the Box to think about it."

"And?" Na'lah swallowed hard. Truth be told, over the past three years, since her brother and his friends were imprisoned, she had smothered the part of herself that might have wanted a relationship. But sometimes, when she was alone and her mind walked the hallways of the past, something deep inside her yearned for Hobler's easy way of listening, his laughter, his scent. There had been no one like him since. Not even close.

"We were good together," he said. "Really good."

Butterflies fluttered in Na'lah's chest, but she tamped them down. "Yeah," she said, tearing into another bite of jerky, "until you ended it." She chewed angrily, her desire for this goblin next to her grappling with the pain he had caused. "Twice."

Hobler shook his head. "By the Mother Tree, really, Na'lah? You're Garak's sister. What did you expect me to do?"

Na'lah leapt to her feet. "Blazing Sky Fire, Hobler! This again?" Her throat strained against the need to shout. "What is it with you and Garak, huh? Who cares what he thinks?"

Hobler lowered his eyes. "He's my captain." He sighed and looked through the oaks and into the valley.

"So what? Is he captain of your heart, too?"

Hobler frowned. "It's... it's complicated."

Na'lah ground her teeth. "You think I don't know that? He's my brother, but I'm my own person. And so are you."

Hobler took a slow breath. "Maybe it's me, but I don't think I could do that to him."

Na'lah threw up her hands. "There you have it."

"There you have it."

A breeze moved through the tops of the oaks, and the leaves rustled, applauding the scene of quarreling lovers below them. A crow flapped away, cawing loudly. Its mate answered from across the valley. Blood pounded in Na'lah's ears. She made tight fists over her fingers to keep them from shaking. *Blazing Sky Fires!* She thought she had buried the pain of losing Hobler long ago, but here it was again, fresh from the grave, stronger than ever. She loomed over him, fists clenched. Now that the issue was out, it was out. She had to see it through. "So, what are we going to do about it this time?"

Hobler gave a light snort. He looked into her eyes and held her in that place where only he could touch her. Through her rage, she felt her heart open just a crack. "I love you, Na'lah. I can't help it. I still love you."

The crack in Na'lah's heart widened, and her desire for this goblin poured out. The strength of her wanting surprised her, despite three years of tamping it down. "I love you, too," she managed through a dry throat. "You already know that."

He smiled then, soft and sad. "I love you, but we can never be together."

The opening in Na'lah's heart snapped shut. "What?"

Hobler shook his head. "I can't do that to Garak, Na'lah. Ever. Relationships are built on trust, and Garak and I need to trust each other."

Na'lah's mouth went dry. "How does us being together affect you and Garak?"

Garak shrugged. "What if he thinks the wrong thing about us? If he thinks we're just, you know?"

"What?"

"You know, in it for fun."

Na'lah sighed. It had been just for fun, at first. Sneaking around behind Garak's back, keeping their times together secret. But relationships have a way of getting serious fast when lives are on the line, and it only took a few training missions together for Na'lah and Hobler to realize they had something more than "just fun" on their hands. Na'lah had found the only person besides Badwin and Papa who saw her for who she was. Saw beyond her skin that was too pale for a goblin and eyes that were far too blue. And Hobler? With Na'lah, he could finally be something other than the gang's meaty fist.

She looked at him, saw the hurt in his eyes as he stared into the valley. That was when it hit her.

He loves Garak.

He loves both *of us.*

Thinking of the way Papa talked whenever Na'lah was mad, she tried coming at the topic from another angle. "Have you ever talked to Garak... about us?"

Hobler's eyes went wide. "What? No! Never!"

"Why not?"

"Well, then he would know."

"And?"

"If he got angry, I would have to choose between you and him."

Fingers of doubt touched Na'lah's heart. She almost didn't want to ask, but she did. "And?"

Hobler closed his eyes. "And then I'd lose him."

Na'lah knelt in the leaves next to Hobler and took his face in her hands. His eyes glistened. She leaned in and kissed his forehead. "You big oaf," she whispered. "You're–"

And then Na'lah froze.

Something was in the woods.

She snatched her bow from the ground. When she touched the string with her missing fingers, she grimaced and flipped the bow to her off-hand.

What is it? Hobler signed, his gaze suddenly sharp and alert. He, too, reached for his bow.

Na'lah peered up the hillside, where the flicker of movement, something dark, had moved between the oaks. She scanned the spaces between trunks, looking for the telltale sign of horizontal lines that would be a deer's back, searching for the angled lines of a crouching elf. At first, she saw nothing. And then, a flock of crows descended into the forest. "There," she breathed, pointing her chin toward a patch of buckthorn. "Someone."

Indeed, it was someone. Someone hooded and cloaked in black, stepping deftly between the trunks of their black oak grove. Hobler leaned from side to side. "I don't see anything."

Na'lah snorted at him lightly. *How could he not see it?* Whoever it was, they weren't trying very hard to stay concealed, but they knew enough to stay just at the edge of visibility through the undergrowth. "Over there," Na'lah whispered. "Now it's slipping behind that fist of granite."

Hobler leaned back and forth. "I don't see anything."

"Are you blind? It's right–" and then Na'lah stopped because the figure stepped into a shaded clearing.

A Spirit Walker.

Na'lah's throat, already dry from her argument with Hobler, cracked. "What is *that* doing here?"

"What? I don't see anything." Hobler leaned in close to her, trying to get her line of vision. "What is it?"

"A Spirit Walker."

And as she voiced the name, the black-robed creature raised its hand, with two mangled fingers, and gestured for Na'lah to come closer. Na'lah tried to swallow, but her throat was too scratchy. "It wants me."

"Are you sure? I don't see anything."

"I don't think you're supposed to."

Hobler looked at her like she was losing her mind. But Na'lah ignored him.

Something pulled at her, and an invisible cord affixed to her chest drew her closer to the thing. She tried to pull back, but the urge to follow the Walker was irresistible. "It's calling me," she whispered, trying not to let the pleading fear infect her voice. She took an unbidden step toward the Spirit Walker. "Hobler, it has me!"

The cloaked figure turned and drifted away, northwards, into the mountains. The invisible, corded connection attached to Na'lah's chest dragged her with it, through the leaves and fallen branches. "Hobler! Help!" She tried not to scream, tried to breathe the way Master Goggins had taught her, but the fingers of panic were tightening their grip on her mind.

Hobler grabbed Na'lah by the waist, strained until the cords in his neck bulged under his gray skin, but even the mighty goblin hunter couldn't stop Na'lah. "Blazing Sky Fires!" Hobler grunted. "What magic is this?"

Over the mountainside, the Spirit Walker dragged Na'lah with Hobler stumbling after, carrying their packs and weapons of war. Over rock and vine, limb and grass, Na'lah tripped after the shadowy figure against her will until they came to a ridge overlooking a deep valley. Na'lah clawed frantically at rocks and shrubs, trying to slow her momentum. Was the Spirit Walker going to throw her off the cliff? Then, as suddenly as it had started, the tugging on her chest vanished, just like the Spirit Walker. Na'lah took a slow breath and let a warm updraft from the valley soothe her quaking nerves. "I'm free," she said to Hobler once he caught up to her. "I don't know why, but it just let me go."

Hobler shook his head. "Great. Now we're half a day off course. We were supposed to head due east. Not north."

"I know, I know." Na'lah squinted into the valley. Hobler was right, of course. Their mission, according to Garak, was to run the edge of the box in their search for Alistar. But what was this Spirit Walker doing in the wilds? She scanned the valley, trying to understand. "Why did you bring me here?" she muttered. "What do you want?"

Hobler, not understanding, huffed. "Look, it wasn't my idea to pair up with you, okay? That was your brother."

Na'lah rolled her eyes. "Blazing Sky Fire, you self-absorbed fool. I was talking to the Spirit Walker."

Hobler grunted. "It's gone?"

Na'lah nodded. "Yeah. But what did it want?" She studied the area, looking for clues. Across the valley, a trio of circling crows dove into the upper branches of a massive tree. Na'lah's eyes went wide in surprise. It was right in front of her. How could she have missed it? She raised her arm and pointed at the tree with her missing fingers. "There, Hobler. That's why the Spirit Walker led me here." She swallowed, almost too amazed to let the

words pass her lips. "A Mother Tree. And not just one... a whole grove."

Hobler followed her gaze. "By all the gods," he whispered, and pressed both hands, palms wide, over his chest, the goblin sign of reverence. "How?"

Na'lah shook her head. "I don't know. I thought Mother Trees only existed in our lands, not with the elves."

"Me too." Hobler plopped down on a rock. His head shook from side to side. "How can there be so many?"

Yes, how could there be so many Mother Trees here? And alive? She looked over the valley of green giants. Mother Trees were at the heart of every goblin city and settlement, but in the years just before Na'lah's birth, one by one, they fell asleep and died. When they died, so did a crucial something in the goblin people's very being. Things had grown dark in Draal since the Mother Tree died there. People were cranky, selfish, and short-tempered. Even the air was different, or so the older goblins said. *It's the only world I've known,* Na'lah thought bitterly.

But here was a way to bring the Mother Trees back to goblinkind.

Was this what Papa wanted her to see?

How did he know?

Something fluttered in Na'lah's chest, something she thought had died that day in the belly of the Mother Tree temple, when she learned the truth about the goblin Elders and Shamanka. "We have to go down there,"

Na'lah breathed, and scampered over the side of the ridge.

"Na'lah!" Hobler called. "What are you doing? We have to go back! Focus on the mission!"

She knew he was right, but something drew Na'lah on. A grove of Mother Trees? She had to walk there, had to bring a story of hope back to her struggling people, back to the temple, back to her mother's frowning face. She slid down the ridge, not taking the time to slow her descent. If the Spirit Walker had led her here, what was there to fear, after all? Wasn't she meant to be here? Hobler scrambled after her, muttering and hissing about staying on track, but Na'lah didn't care.

Soon, she was on the valley's floor, running past young Mother Trees, letting her arms go wide so her fingers could touch their rough bark as she passed. How could there be so many Mother Trees in one place when in the goblin lands they always grew alone?

Then, she came to the largest tree of all, a mighty Mother Tree that dwarfed all the rest, its trunk so wide it would have taken twenty goblins touching fingertips to encircle its base. Na'lah breathed a sigh of amazement and put her hand on its thick bark. Something tingled under her fingertips. "Hobler, come touch."

She pressed her hand into the rough creases of the bark. Something flowed through her. Something powerful. Despite their recent fight, she wanted nothing more than to feel this with Hobler. "Hobler?"

Na'lah heard a whirl and then a thump. Still touching the Mother Tree, she turned to find Hobler clutching his side. He looked at her, eyes wide with surprise. "Na'lah?" Then he collapsed.

Na'lah's free hand went to the hilt of her father's sword. Before she could draw it, a familiar voice from the underbrush made the stumps of Na'lah's missing fingers twitch. "Well, well, well. Look who we have here."

12

A Friendly Reunion With My Old Kidnapper

Na'lah slowly removed her hand from the Mother Tree. The electric feeling left her like a punch to the gut. She gasped, trying to catch her breath. The tingling ebbed away. She shook her head to quiet the swarm of bees buzzing in her mind. Hobler was down, and the individual who did it was behind her—a skilled individual to get a jump on both of them.

How to escape?

The feral part of her screamed to *Run! Run! Run!* But something stopped her. The memory of leaving Badwin raced through her head. She couldn't make that mistake again. She would save Hobler, even at the cost of her own life.

She turned.

The hilt of a dagger protruded from Hobler's right side. Bright crimson spilled from his ribs and pooled on the soil beneath him. She knew that color well. A darker red would have meant a vital strike. Hobler was safe for now, but the gap was wide. Too much blood had already left his body. The knife was holding back a river but could not dam the flow. Na'lah let out a small breath. She had to patch him up quickly if Hobler was going to survive.

A shadow carrying a short hunting bow emerged from the forest, slim and certain, like a mountain cat circling its prey. The figure was clearly female, given the slender curve of her hips. Elven, considering her height. A calm, female voice spoke. "Well, Na'lah, we keep running into each other. Luck is on my side. And I see you brought a friend." The female snorted lightly. "I do not like surprises."

Na'lah went rigid. She knew that voice. That voice stole into her city. That voice took two of her fingers. That voice demanded Na'lah play by her rules.

A sturdy elf with calculating eyes stood over Hobler's crumpled form. The easy way the elf's hands rested on the sword hilts hanging from her belt showed she had been trained. Honed to fight. Prepared to kill. She wore a tunic bearing an emerald chevron on her chest. Na'lah's stomach twisted. This was no ordinary hunter, but a captain of rangers, the elite elven hunters. Captains generally stayed close to the Elders, acting as bodyguards instead of scouts. They oversaw elven rangers but never went into the woods with them. So, why had this one been in Draal? And why would she want Alistar dead? And why was she here, under this Mother Tree, now?

Na'lah clenched her fist until her nails dug into her palm. She would love nothing more than to run this elf through with her blade, but the elf's companions were no doubt hiding among the trees. Na'lah's eyes stayed trained on this ranger before her, but her ears strained for any sound that would clue her in as to how many rangers were hidden in the forest. "What have you done?"

The elf nudged Hobler's crumpled form with her boot. "Hmm. He's a big one, isn't he? Don't worry. He should be fine as long as you cooperate. I wanted to have a private conversation, Na'lah. That's all. No interruptions." The elf tightened her grip on the two shortswords hanging from her hip. An empty sheath for a dagger dangled from her belt.

Na'lah glanced at the dagger in Hobler's side and scowled. "What do you want to talk about?" Na'lah hissed, barely daring to breathe. Her mind screamed to take action, but with Hobler lying there, she did not want to test this situation yet.

"I just wanted to inquire about your mission, Na'lah. Alistar is still breathing, and time is running short." The elf's voice was flat, cold, and lethal. Every word was like a thrust of a knife. Na'lah's instincts roared at her to grab the elf's throat and squeeze the life from her, but she fought the urge. The elf was testing her.

Na'lah's nails dug deeper into her palm. The small prick of pain was the only thing that kept her body in check. "Why do you think I am in your lands, elf? Sightseeing? I am going to complete your mission, and then I am coming back for you. That is a promise."

"I would expect nothing less, Na'lah. Just make sure your mind is still focused on killing Alistar. Don't get distracted, perhaps by a missing sibling?" The elf glanced down at Hobler and slowly walked towards Na'lah. "Remember, I do not like surprises." She stopped a few strides short of Na'lah. With a very slow movement, her eyes measured Na'lah from head to toe and back again.

Na'lah felt like cattle at the market. "Killing someone like Alistar isn't easy. I needed a new spotter since you have my brother captive. Now, you've removed him. You also graciously removed two of my fingers, making the shot even more difficult."

"Not my concern, Na'lah. Now, put your hands down. You look foolish."

Na'lah dropped her hands to her side, but she still stood rigid. No need to antagonize this elf any further. Besides, Na'lah still wasn't sure if this elf was alone, despite hearing nothing from the brush to indicate companions. *She is here by herself? Bold.* Na'lah needed to speed up this little conversation if she was going to tend to Hobler and rescue her brother.

The elf continued. "I have been tracking you since you crossed the border. Just remember, I can find you anywhere you go. I think I proved that back in Draal," she cooed while wagging a finger in front of Na'lah. "But now I have a bigger question. What would a goblin hunter be doing in our sacred grove? You veered from your original path and headed this way at the last moment. A bit out of the way, wouldn't you say?"

Panic rose in Na'lah's chest. She felt small and powerless, like a newborn goblin at its mother's side. She frowned. "Are we done?"

The elf passed Na'lah and walked to the Mother Tree. She placed her hand on the bark and closed her eyes for a moment. Na'lah watched her for any sign of the feeling she had received from touching the tree, but there was nothing. The elf slowly opened her eyes and turned towards Na'lah.

"Magnificent, aren't they? It is odd you found this place, or that you foolishly stumbled upon it. We have kept this valley a secret for many generations. Ahman'Dur. It is sacred to our people. To me," she sighed. "They are not just big trees in a valley, you know." She waved her hand around. "They are sacred, have magic under all this." She rapped a knuckle against the trunk. "It sleeps now, but it is foretold it will wake once the chosen one returns. And when that elf arrives, we will have the power we need to finally put an end to goblinkind."

She walked back towards Na'lah, glancing at the lump that was Hobler. She stopped and paused for a moment. "Alistar takes his monthly journeys close to this valley, visiting villages on the outskirts," the elf said, examining her nails. "He believes this valley is the key to the Elves' balance with nature. I believe he is an idiot. The Mother Trees are the key to victory in our war with your kind. These trees will give us the final edge we need." She snapped her eyes to Na'lah and studied her. "You were headed for Granndor, the village Alistar was in until you abruptly stopped and headed right for this valley. This tells me one of two things."

"I am guessing you are going to enlighten me?"

The elf held up a finger. "One, you took an incredibly fortunate detour." She held up another finger. "Or two, you have others with you besides this lump of a goblin. Either way, Na'lah, I have made it perfectly clear that I do not like surprises. Finish the mission, or your brother and these incompetent friends of yours will not make it home."

The elf tossed an object at Na'lah's face. On instinct, Na'lah swiped it out of the air. When she looked back, the elf was gone. She looked in her hand and found a sheath for the dagger in Hobler's side. She spared a quick moment to scan the surroundings before crouching next to Hobler. She cradled his head in her lap. Tenderly, she put a finger to the side of his neck to feel for a pulse. Faint, but beating.

"You overgrown idiot. Don't die on me."

Still with his head in her lap, she grabbed his adventure pack and rummaged to find the yarrow pouch. Balling up a fistful of the leaves in her right hand, she put her left hand on the hilt of the dagger. With one swift motion, she yanked the dagger out and jammed the powdered leaf into the wound.

A small grunt escaped from Hobler's mouth, and his eyelids fluttered. "Good," Na'lah whispered. "Pain means you're not dead yet." She sat stroking his forehead for a moment until exhaustion from the day's events took over. Seeing Hobler breathing softly, Na'lah leaned back and rested her head against the massive trunk of the tree.

A prickling sensation tingled the back of her scalp. It built quickly and then surged through her whole body. Na'lah gasped. The weariness faded as the tingling built. Her eyes flared wide. The glade brightened. Ash leaves rippled silver overhead. The breeze carried the scent of running water... a stream... not far off. Papa's blade hummed in its sheath, a steady rhythm growing stronger and stronger. Na'lah touched the hilt. "Magic?"

Hobler moaned and rolled his head to the side, his breathing coming quicker. She leaned forward. "Hobler? Can you hear me?"

She pulled away from the tree to check his wounds. The prickling in her scalp faded almost immediately. The muscles in her neck felt heavy, like wet wool. Exhaustion washed over Na'lah, and Hobler's breathing slowed. Curious, she leaned back again. As soon as the back of her head touched the massive Mother Tree, the tingling returned, and Hobler's breathing increased.

Na'lah's mind raced. An idea hit her. Slowly, she stood up, making sure not to shake him. She threw the adventure pack onto her back and grabbed him under the arms. Carefully, as not to jar the wound too much, she dragged him towards the mighty Mother Tree. Once there, she dropped the pack off to the side and sat down at the base of the tree. She leaned into it, and the feeling coursed through her, stronger this time. The fatigue dropped away. Her senses opened to the world around her.

She closed her eyes and sighed, allowing the feeling to warm her, put her at ease, and rejuvenate her. Papa's sword buzzed calmly at her side. She put her hand on the hilt. Images of Papa when he was younger flitted through her mind's eye. The tingling wrapped tightly about her, protecting her from the outside world. Na'lah smiled, despite herself. Was this magic? Was this tingling the hand of the gods, like Mother and Papa used to talk about? Echoes of her fight with her mother, about the Mother Tree temple and the dances of the Shamanka, replayed in her ear. Had Mother been right all along? Pressure built behind her eyes. Her chin trembled. Na'lah cleared her throat and wiped her eyes with the back of her wrist. It was too much to think about. She needed to focus on the mission.

She stayed like that for a few moments, breathing easily. Finally, she leaned forward and pulled Hobler's head into her lap again. The tingling from the tree grew until the prickling covered her entire body. Hobler gasped, eyes shooting open. He turned his head towards her.

"Na'lah. I need to tell you that..." He faded, eyes closing again. His breathing became regular.

Na'lah rubbed his forehead gently. Something about this tingling was making it to Hobler. Was it healing him? *Yes, but will it be enough?*

A pair of crows settled in a copse of ash trees to the south. They watched her with their black eyes, reminding Na'lah she was not alone in these woods. "This is taking too long," she muttered. "We need to get you up, buddy."

Hobler's breathing grew steady. She carefully rose, resting him against the massive trunk. She crawled to the adventure pack and rummaged through it. She pulled out a cloak held together with patches of faded greens and browns. The way the colors were arranged, the cloak blended into most natural settings. It was the same cloak all hunters had when they were on missions.

She wrapped the cloak around Hobler, stepping back to see her handy work. When she was satisfied that Hobler blended in well enough, she crouched at his side. "I'll be right back," she whispered. "I want a better look at this valley."

She jogged through Ahman'Dur, examining the rows and rows of the sacred trees, amazed at how many there were. At the base of a bluff, she started to climb. It was not a challenging climb, but with two digits missing, it was hard enough to bring sweat beading down her face. A few times, she grabbed crevasses in the rock, thinking she had full facility of her hand, only to slip, unleashing a cascade of debris cracking and crumbling to the valley floor.

Finally, she made the peak. Sweat stung her eyes. When she looked back, she gasped. She could see the whole valley from this height. The Mother Trees were protected on all sides by cliffs. The Great Mother, where she had left Hobler, stood proudly in the center of the grove. It towered over the others, stretching her weighty arms to protect her children. Na'lah had just been amongst those magnificent trees but seeing them from this vantage point took her breath away. And then, for the first time in three years, Na'lah touched the tips of her fingers to her forehead, and then to her chest.

After a moment, Na'lah tore her eyes from the majestic sight. She scanned the valley surrounding Ahman'Dur. It was ingenious, a perfect hiding spot for this treasured grove.

A small plume of smoke rose into the air a distance away. A village? *Good*, thought Na'lah. *That must be Granndor.* With a direction in mind, she made her descent from the cliff and hurried back to Hobler.

It took her a bit longer to get down the face of the bluff than she expected. By the time she was at the base, darkness had settled over the grove. She hastened to get back. Soon, Na'lah saw the huge trunk where she left

Hobler and went into a sprint. He was still asleep when she found him. "Hobler," she said, softly shaking him. "Hobler, wake up. I know where we're going."

No response.

She shook him with more force, dread trickling down her spine. "You stupid big oaf. I can't have you holding me back. I need to get to Badwin! Blazing Sky Fire, open your eyes!"

A crow squawked above, and Hobler's eyes shot wide open. "Na'lah!" he screamed, grabbing her by the front of her tunic and yanking her down.

"What in the name of the Mother Tree are you...?"

A whistling sound and then a thump rang out above Na'lah... right where her head had been.

13

Out Of The Frying Pan

Na'lah craned her neck to find an elven hunting arrow quivering in the Mother Tree's thick bark. She threw herself over Hobler like a lanky spider and scanned the deep shadows of the sacred grove. "Who's here now?" she growled, reaching for the bow slung over her shoulder. "Show yourself," Na'lah called. "Let's get this over with."

Leaves rustled from all sides of the grove as six elven rangers, short bows drawn, bloomed from the underbrush. "Great," Na'lah muttered to Hobler, whose eyes had fluttered and then closed again, "a hunting party."

One of the masked rangers moved forward a little. "Goblins? In the Grove of Ahman'Dur?" The ranger, a male by his voice, relaxed the tension of his bow and held his free hand against his chest, a motion not unsimilar to the goblin gesture of reverence. Despite the

146

elf's respect for the Mother Tree, the set of his eyes lay hard against Na'lah. "What are you doing here?" the elven ranger asked. He drew his bow back again, the deadly tip trained on Na'lah's heart.

Na'lah ground her teeth. She could escape this hunting party. There were only, what, six elves? And she was ready this time. They weren't going to jump her like back in Draal. But what about Hobler? Her mind flashed to the way she abandoned her brother to the elves. She would not make that mistake again. The lead elf shuffled forward and lifted his well-aimed arrow toward Na'lah's face. "Speak," the elven ranger demanded, "or you and your gray friend die at my command!"

Na'lah dropped her short bow and raised her hands. She sat back on her haunches and studied her captors. "My friend and I were hunting deer. We didn't realize we were in elven lands."

"What's wrong with your friend?"

Na'lah glanced at Hobler, still asleep under the hunter's cloak that hid his injury. "He's wounded. A hunting accident."

"Lies," another elf muttered. "What did you expect, Sylvan?"

"Kill them and be done with it," growled a third ranger.

The leader, Sylvan, kept his eyes and arrow trained on Na'lah. "No goblin has ever set foot on the sacred ground of Ahman'Dur. The penalty is death."

Na'lah slowly put her hands down. It was not too late. Crouched as she was, a quick leap to the side could win her the cover of the younger Mother Trees not three strides away. She risked a quick glance at the dense saplings. Just as her eyes touched the mottled light of the underbrush, the ranger's bowstring twanged, and an arrow sprouted not a handbreadth from Na'lah's knee. "Don't even think about it," the elf hissed.

"What are we waiting for?" the second elf asked. "They desecrated sacred ground."

"Agreed," came the third voice again. "Let their blood serve as a sacrifice."

Na'lah leaned against the roots of the massive Mother Tree. How could things get any worse? Here she was, deep in elven territory in the middle of a Mother Tree grove, a secret that could save her people, could revive goblinkind... but to get that information back, she would have to sacrifice Hobler. She ran her fingers over the rough bark of the Mother Tree's roots. "Please wake up," she whispered. "I need you." Would that strange feeling come back? The one that seemed to heal Hobler earlier? Her heart thumped wildly in her chest, and she fought the urge to break for the safety of the trees.

No tingle came, so she slowly took one hand and placed it over the sticky mess of Hobler's weeping wound beneath the cloak. The yarrow packing must have come loose because the dagger wound was bleeding again. "Please," Na'lah breathed. "Don't let him die." Images of their time together, wrapped in one another's arms, his warm breath against the skin of her neck, flitted through her mind's eye. Despite their recent fight, something in the pit of her gut told her they could work things out, that they were meant for one another, if only he could survive.

But then her training raised its head. For years, she had trained under Master Goggins to learn the ways of the hunter. How to walk without being seen. How to speak with her hands. How to move like a shadow.

How to kill.

And most important of all, how to put the needs of goblinkind above all else. Being a hunter meant sacrificing personal desires for the greater good. Maybe that's what Hobler had been trying to say. Maybe that's why they couldn't be together.

A horrible realization came to Na'lah.

If the goblins of Draal were ever to learn about the valley of the Mother Trees, if they were ever to resurrect the Mother Tree temples, Na'lah had to abandon Hobler to the elves.

Now.

If Hobler was awake, if he could talk, he would tell her the same thing. The life of one goblin against the knowledge that more Mother Trees existed in an elven valley? The bitterness of the answer filled Na'lah's mouth with the taste of copper. And hadn't the Spirit Walker warned Na'lah that she would lose three things that were close to her? What could be closer than this goblin she had once loved? She squeezed Hobler's side with one hand and dug her nails into the Mother Tree's roots with the other. "Forgive me," she whispered to Hobler, knowing what she had to do. "I can't protect you."

Just then, something shivered in the ridged bark of the Mother Tree's roots. Na'lah edged away. Did the roots just wriggle? The elven ranger growled. "What are you up to, goblin?"

Na'lah shook her head and shot her hands in the air. "Nothing! I... I don't understand!"

The ground crumbled beneath Hobler. Spindly fingers of roots sprang from the ground and wove themselves into a damp netting around the wounded hunter. His eyes shot open. "Na'lah?"

Hobler's body tensed against the roots, but they were too many and too strong. He strained and growled. Veins and thick muscles corded in his neck beneath his rich, gray skin. "What's happening?" he panted.

Several roots stretched toward his straining mouth. Hobler arched his neck, fighting to keep the roots from creeping down his throat. His efforts were not enough. The roots tugged like spider fingers at the cusp of his lips, inch wormed over his teeth, and having won a solid purchase on his tongue, galloped full down his throat. Hobler's eyes rolled wide and white. Then, as suddenly as it had started, his eyes fogged over, and he collapsed into unconsciousness.

"Hobler!" Na'lah screamed and clutched at his body, but the mighty goblin hunter did not, could not respond.

No one moved as Na'lah and the elven rangers stared at the entwined goblin.

The ground beneath Hobler groaned and opened like an ancient maw. Thick roots, like teeth and tongues, dangled over the darkening pit. Before her horrified eyes, the roots dragged Hobler into the grim grave and snapped shut, trapping Hobler beneath the loamy forest floor.

Silence fell on the sacred glade. Somewhere to the east, a crow called. There, to the west, a crow answered. Na'lah stared at the ground that had swallowed Hobler. The area, barren of leaves, was churned like a row in a garden. Or a grave. She blinked. How could he be gone that quickly? Then, she remembered. "The Spirit Walker's prophecy," she whispered.

Had it come to this? To tempt her with visions of rekindled love, only to have it immediately snatched away? Her vision swirled and her gut churned. Was she going to throw up? Na'lah lifted her eyes to the elves.

Her captors, bows still drawn, stared at her, their eyes narrow. "What have you done, goblin?" Sylvan asked.

"What? I didn't do anything! It was the tree! The Mother Tree took Hobler!"

One of the rangers edged closer to his captain. "The Great Mother... we all saw it. She came alive." He loosened the pressure on his bow, allowing him to press a freed hand to his chest.

"The Great Mother *is* life, you fool."

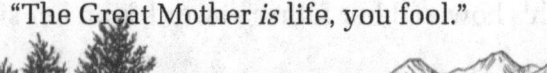

"You know what I mean. It moved. We must tell the Elders." He drew back his bow again and aimed it at Na'lah. "The Elders need to question this one."

Sylvan glared at Na'lah. "What are you? You're too pale to be a goblin. And your eyes... too blue."

"I'm... I'm... nobody." She looked at the loose soil where Hobler had vanished. "Please. You have to help me get him back."

The leader snorted. "We'll see about that." He lifted his chin at two of his companions. "Take her weapons and bind her, whatever she is. The Elders will decide what to make of all this."

"What? No! We have to save Hobler!" Na'lah's mind whirled. Part of her, the part drilled into her mind during her training as a hunter, screamed at her to dive into the underbrush, disappear, and flee back to goblin lands to share the secrets of the Mother Tree grove. But another part, a growing shadow, loomed large over her thoughts. What was this web she was being drawn into? Why would the Spirit Walker have led her here only to lose Hobler so quickly? Was this part of some grand plan from beyond the Gray Mist?

"That goblin got what he deserved."

"No!" Na'lah scratched at the ground with her nails, shredding the soil that had swallowed Hobler. "Hobler!"

Two elven rangers stormed to Na'lah's side. They snatched her by the arms and bound her wrists behind her back with thick leather straps. Another pair of elves took Na'lah's bow and her father's sword from her side.

"On your feet, dog," one of them growled. "I've no love of goblins, if that's what you are, much less one that desecrated holy ground. Why the Mother Tree would defile itself with the blood of your friend is beyond me." He tossed Papa's sword to the ranger captain. "Here. Take a look at that."

The leader half drew the short sword. His eyes narrowed. "Interesting. What's a goblin doing with an elven sword? Elisara will want to see this." Then, to the elves restraining Na'lah, he said, "Gag and blind her. I don't want that thing causing any more problems."

The elves used another strap of leather to roughly gag Na'lah, the cordage biting into the corners of her mouth. They yanked her to her feet and tied a piece of cloth over her eyes to serve as a blindfold. The sharp tip of a sword probed her in the back. Not enough to draw blood, but more than enough to get Na'lah to step forward. "Move," the elf grunted. "We'll keep you on track." He paused. "Mostly."

Their hike through elven lands took forever. Blindfolded as she was, Na'lah had to rely on her other senses as she had been trained. At first, she counted her steps, using the methodic numbering as a tool to calm her hammering heart. *Thirty-one. Thirty-two. Thirty-three.* She focused on the ground beneath her feet as it changed from leafy and flat to rocky and steep. *We're climbing out of the valley,* Na'lah realized. *Probably heading to that village I saw from the ridge.*

A crow called from overhead as they marched. Another answered. *Are they following us?* Na'lah wondered. The trained hunter part of her mind barked at her to stay focused on the details of her surroundings, but there were still many questions. What had happened to Hobler? Was he gone forever? Why had the Spirit Walker led her to that grove of Mother Trees only to be caught by an elven patrol?

The questions made her ears buzz. She wanted nothing more than to break free of these thoughts about the Mother Tree, to be the Na'lah she had always wanted to be: the best hunter her people had ever known. But she had promised Papa, and these accursed questions kept piling on. What would her mother say about an entire grove of Mother Trees in elven lands? What would she say about the tingling from the tree? And what about the elves showing reverence to the largest of the Mother Trees? Did elves have a spiritual connection to the Mother Trees, just like goblinkind? And if so, what did that mean for the war between their people?

Somewhere ahead, a dog barked, followed by the tinkling laughter of an elven child. The comforting scent of cooking fires came to Na'lah's keen sense of smell on a warm updraft. They were close to the village now. Very close. The path beneath Na'lah's feet smoothed out. *A road,* she surmised, and then snorted. *No need to count steps now. I'll learn my fate soon enough.*

The sounds of a lively village were all around her. The high-pitched, rhythmic pinging of a blacksmith's hammer on an anvil. The croaking groan of axles beneath a heavily laden merchant's wagon. The chatter of neighbors gossiping. And the hailing cries of a returning hunting party, bearing with them the prize of a captured goblin hunter. Na'lah felt the heat of the sun lessen on her exposed skin and smelled the ashy scent of charred logs. *We're next to the village gate,* she thought. *A village with a wooden wall.* She tucked that piece of intelligence into a corner of her mind for when she would need it later. "Well met, soldier," came an elven male's voice. *A guard at the gatehouse?* "You're back early."

Sylvan grunted. "We stopped at Ahman'Dur to pray and found this," he yanked Na'lah forward by the elbow, "and another goblin at the foot of the Great Mother."

"That's a goblin? Seems too pale to be a goblin. And look at its ears. Almost standing straight up, not flat. You sure that's a goblin?"

"Some kind of freak or something," came the captain's reply. "Anyway, we found it and another goblin at the foot of the Great Mother."

"The Great Mother? What were they doing there?"

"We don't know yet, but strange things happened. Send a messenger to the Elders. They will know what to do with this one."

"Where's the other goblin?"

"That's part of the story. Now, get that message to the Elders."

There was a scampering of feet ahead of Na'lah as the messengers scurried away. "Move," the soldier said, and yanked Na'lah forward.

Voices whispered around her, young and old. Na'lah turned her ears from side to side, trying to hear what they were saying, but there were too many, talking too fast. "A goblin ghost!"

"A hunter!"

"Will there be a hanging?"

Na'lah's spine stiffened at that. *A hanging?* Why would the Spirit Walker have led her to her death? Na'lah's heart pounded. She began counting her steps again. *One. Two. Three.*

The voices built as they moved to what Na'lah assumed would be the center of the village. Sylvan walked beside Na'lah, his firm grip ever on Na'lah's elbow. Eventually, the elven captain dragged Na'lah up a flight of stairs. "Stand here," he growled, and yanked the blindfold from Na'lah's eyes.

She was on a wooden platform overlooking the village square. A circle of huts ringed the village center, surrounded by great trees with platforms and houses built into the branches overhead. Elves of all ages crowded into the meeting space. From the size of the crowd, Na'lah guessed around two to three hundred souls had gathered to see her, but the number of homes she saw at first glance couldn't have housed that many elves. Why were so many elves in such a small village?

A gong sounded, and a procession of elven warriors clad in finely forged chain mail led seven ancient elves to the platform. They were old, these elves, with deep wrinkles and knowing eyes. One of the women, an ancient hag shriveled like a mid-winter apple, scowled at Na'lah as a young ranger helped her mount the platform's stairs. The old Elder spat at Na'lah's feet as she passed. "Dog," the silver-haired elf muttered.

Villagers gathered and pressed against the raised platform as the Elders took their places on finely carved wooden chairs, brought forward just for the occasion. The elven warriors who had appeared with the elven Elders, some sort of honor guard apparently, took places behind the Elders. Na'lah scanned their faces and froze. *Her!* Na'lah's throat tightened into a knot when she saw the elven warrior from the Mother Tree grove, the same elf who had broken into her house, taken her fingers, and stuck Hobler with a dagger, scowling directly at her. Na'lah opened her mouth to acknowledge the elf, to let her know she was trying to finish the mission, but a slight shake of the head from the female warrior told Na'lah to keep her tongue... for now.

Sylvan, who claimed Na'lah as his prize in the Mother Tree grove, raised his hands. "My people, I have summoned you to bear witness to the testimony I lay before the feet of our Elders. I come before you as neither judge nor jury, but as the voice of one who has seen something unexplainable. Listen as I report what my hunting party and I experienced at the foot of the

Great Mother. Listen to our Elders as they pass judgment on this trespassing goblin."

A hush fell over the crowd as the captain related the events in the sacred grove of Mother Trees: The elven hunting party went to the grove seeking blessings from the Great Mother before they went on patrol. They were surprised to see two goblins at the foot of the Great Mother. The strange-looking goblin, Na'lah, seemed to be praying. The other, injured, lay just behind her. As the hunting party confronted the goblins, the Great Mother wrapped her roots about the wounded goblin and drew him into the earth.

The crowd leaned toward the platform, soaking in the elf's story. When he mentioned Na'lah praying at the foot of the Great Mother, several gasps rent the silence. When the ranger finished his tale, the old elven woman, the one who had scowled and spat at Na'lah's feet, leaned on her staff and stood on shaking knees. "Sylvan, we, the Council of Elders, hear your words." The Elder touched aged fingers to her cracked lips and then to her ears. "Our gratitude for your report and for bringing to us this," she cast a withering scowl upon Na'lah, "abomination." She paused and surveyed the gathering. Then, "A goblin on sacred ground? What more needs to be said? My people, the Great Mother has spoken through her actions. If we were meant to show mercy, the Great Mother would have shown mercy to this goblin's partner. As it were, the Great Mother has devoured the wounded one, ridding the world of his stain and showing us the path we must follow." The ancient elf leaned heavily on her staff and worked her way to the front of the platform. Half turning, she thrust a bent finger in Na'lah's direction. "Tomorrow, this goblin hangs!"

The crowd erupted in support. Na'lah leaned away from the shouting, her mind reeling. "No! You don't understand! I was praying to the Great Mother! Just like you!"

The ancient elf wheeled and delivered a stinging backhand to Na'lah's face. "Silence!"

Na'lah fell backwards and collapsed to her knees. Her ears rang, but she had sense enough about her to hear the crowd's roaring diminish to a grumbling murmur. She shook away the pain to see elven heads in the crowd moving aside as someone passed through them, someone a bit taller than most elves, but not tall enough for Na'lah to see exactly who it was. Finally, the crowd parted, and an elf armored in the fine chain armor of his kind stepped to the platform stairs. His head was crowned with chestnut hair. His cheekbones, fine and high, served to frame calm, calm eyes. Moreover, this elven warrior's sword arm was in a sling. Na'lah raised her gaze to the warrior and looked Alistar Elithium dead in the eyes.

Alistar mounted the platform in the middle of the elven village, bowed low to the Council of Elders, and then came to stand before Na'lah of the Short Bow. Squatting low, he leaned forward, grabbed Na'lah by her head, and pulled her close. "Follow my lead," he whispered in her ear, "and we may yet be able to save both your friend and your brother."

14

All The World's A Stage

Alistar shoved Na'lah's head back down. Clumps of hair fell across her face, shielding her eyes from the crowd, but allowing her to peek through the strands. Alistar studied Na'lah before turning to the villagers. He paused, taking in the sight before him. The crowd hushed and leaned in.

The ancient Elder stood to Alistar's side. At her side was the female elf who had broken into Na'lah's house. The female leaned toward the ancient Elder and whispered in her ear. The Elder's mouth bent into a bitter scowl. Tension radiated off the ancient one, but after listening to whatever Na'lah's assailant told her, the old elf relaxed.

Alistar raised his hands. "My people, every year I travel to the villages surrounding Ahman'Dur. I have been the Advisor, the Protector, and the Caregiver for the Great Trees for many years, as appointed by the

Council of Elders." At this, he locked eyes with the old Elder. He held her gaze longer, daring her to object. She did not, and he maintained eye contact. "I am to have final say as to what happens in the Grove, am I not? Is this not what the Council tasked me with so many moons ago?"

Na'lah shifted her gaze to the Elder and saw her lips curl slightly towards Alistar. The old elf's eyes burned with hatred, but it was gone before anyone besides Na'lah could notice.

"You are respected above all else for the Grove's protection, Alistar. That is not questioned. Villages sing praises of your kind heart and willingness to sacrifice time and effort for the Grove. But this is not about the protection of Ahman'Dur. This," she turned and whipped a bony finger at Na'lah, "is an act of war from the goblin race! This has become a concern for the Council of Elders. This surpasses even your authority, Alistar. We must ready for war." She whacked her staff against the platform and started to walk off the stage.

The crowd gathered and cheered. Some of the elves in the front, loggers, by the adzes over their shoulders, pointed at Na'lah with hatred in their eyes. A rock flew from the crowd and bounced off Na'lah's shoulder. She locked eyes with the elf who had broken into her house and saw a sly smile split her face.

It hit Na'lah just then. *She wanted me to kill Alistar to start a war. But me being captured in the middle of their sacred grove will accomplish the same thing.*

The Elder continued down the steps and into the crowd. Her guard gave Na'lah one last smirk before quickly turning and following her charge closely, leaving Alistar and Na'lah behind on the stage. Na'lah stood in silent horror. *Have I just started a war?*

"Alistar," Na'lah whispered in desperation.

Alistar motioned her to be quiet while he glared at the back of the old hag's head. He waited, standing erect like a statue. His head shifted to the right ever so slightly, a slight smile on his face. Alistar strolled to the front of the stage and paused. "Excuse me for a moment, esteemed Elder, but may I ask a question?"

Slowly the Elder turned, annoyance written across her face. "Yes, what do you wish to discuss now, Alistar Grove Tender? My time is precious, now that we are preparing for war."

"Apologies, Elder, this question is not directed towards you." Alistar's smile grew. "It is for your captain, Elisara."

Elisara, the elven ranger who had long been harassing Na'lah, raised an eyebrow. "Me?"

"Yes, you. The group that found this goblin, they report to you, correct?"

So that is her name, Na'lah thought, *and she is a captain. This explains much.*

At this, Elisara stiffened. "Yes, the rangers of Ahman'Dur report to me. What of it?"

"If I recall their report about what happened in the grove," Alistar continued, "Sylvan, one of your most trustworthy rangers, reported that this goblin seemed to be praying at the base of the Mother tree. Is that correct?"

"That was the report, yes. But we all know goblins are faithless."

"Yes, yes. We all know these," he swept his hand towards Na'lah, "goblin dogs know nothing about the Mother Tree and its power. We have been taught that since we could walk." Alistar made his way off the stage and towards the Elder Council member, never taking his eyes off the captain. The crowd parted before him. "And if I remember correctly, they said the tree wrapped itself around her companion and brought him into the ground?"

"Yes, the Great Mother Tree was protecting us. Do you have a point?"

"And did your hunters observe these two for a time before they engaged?"

"Yes, of course. That is standard procedure."

The villagers mumbled.

"And their account said the tree wrapped itself around the goblin when your rangers confronted the intruders and not before, correct?"

"Where are you going with this?"

Alistar stole a glance at the Council Elder, who was grinding her staff into the ground. Alistar continued, "Your ranger also reported that they initially went into Ahman'Dur to receive the Great Tree's Blessing. Has the Great Tree ever reacted to you or any of your rangers like this before?"

"Of course not. You know the Great Mothers have been dormant for years. The blessing is..."

The Elder grabbed Elisara's wrist and tugged her away from the conversation. "Come, you foolish girl."

"So, one could say that the goblin's presence did not cause a reaction from the Mother Tree. Rather, the Mother Tree reacted when the rangers, your rangers, entered the Grove."

The crowd whispered amongst themselves.

"Of course. The reaction was obviously to protect them from these foul creatures."

"Or, perhaps the Mother Tree was protecting the injured goblin when your rangers strode into view armed... maybe answering a goblin prayer?"

The Elder scoffed. "The Great Tree answering a goblin prayer? This is ridiculous, even for you, Alistar." She tugged Elisara away.

"But the reaction of the Great Mother Tree happened after you engaged, weapons drawn."

"So?" The captain stood her ground, shaking off the Elder's hand.

"Hmm... with that thought, Elder, it seems that the Great Tree has awoken from centuries of rest because of this goblin, and that means this matter supersedes the Council. If there are no objections, Elder, I would like the goblin prisoner brought to my tent, guarded of course, for questioning. And bring her equipment. There might be something there that can help us understand what she was doing in the Grove."

The Elder snatched Elisara's wrist and yanked her from the scene.

"Oh, and Elder," Alistar shouted over the murmuring of the crowd.

"What now?"

"Let's not plan your little war just yet."

Na'lah watched with wide eyes. Not only was she going to breathe for a few more moments, Alistar was creating an opportunity for them to be alone.

A chance to finish the mission!

Her mind raced as to why Alistar had just spared her from a quick death. She was glaring at him, trying to understand his motives, when two guards dragged her and pulled her bodily down the stage, her feet bouncing off each step.

They brought her to a tent a short way from the village. To Na'lah, it seemed quite plain for a figure such as Alistar. There was a simple cot off to one side and a small round rug with a rough table and two chairs facing each other. A single chest squatted in the corner. It wasn't elaborate. It was ordinary, a common chest anyone could buy in Draal's market. A small lamp hung from the center pole and illuminated the tiny space. Other than that, the tent was sparse, bare, and boring.

The guards forced Na'lah into a chair and bound her legs to the chair posts with coarse rope. Once her legs were secured, they put several loops around her chest and tied her to the chair's back. When they were

finished, the guards took silent positions just behind Na'lah.

A few moments later, Alistar pulled the flap of the tent aside. Ducking and entering, he strode straight to the chair opposite Na'lah and took a seat. He stared at her and then turned to the guards. "You can leave us now."

"But sir, we are not to leave her side." The guard eyed Na'lah. "She's dangerous."

"You haven't done a sufficient job securing her? Because if that is the case, maybe we need to find someone new for this position." The guards squirmed. Alistar continued. "As I said before, you may leave us and stand guard outside. If you hear me screaming, by all means, return and save me."

The guards scowled at Na'lah but left to position themselves outside the tent's door.

"You may close the flap now," Alistar called.

There was a grunt, and then the flap cascaded down, leaving Alistar and Na'lah alone in the small space. They stared at one another in silence.

"What did you mean when you said you could save my brother and my friend?" Na'lah asked, finally splitting the silence.

"Keep your voice down. There are wandering ears about."

"Fine. What is this about? I'm a goblin. Your enemy. Why not let them kill me?"

Alistar took a breath. "I believe you are 'The Blended,' Na'lah." Alistar got up and went to the chest in the corner of the tent.

"'The Blended' what? What does that even mean? I might have just caused a war."

"No, Na'lah. The Blended is the one to prevent a war from ever happening." He bent down, pulled a key from around his neck, and unlocked the chest. He drew out a tattered book and placed it on the table. Alistar dragged the table over to the chairs so Na'lah could see. The book was old, ancient maybe. Its cover was cracked and faded by age and featured the engraving of a tree on the cover. Yellow, tinted pages hung between the covers like dusty tongues.

"What is this?" Na'lah asked.

"This, Na'lah, is our history," Alistar stated.

"What do you mean by... ours?"

"Exactly that. The elves and goblins' history a few centuries ago."

Na'lah looked closer and saw it was not a simple tree but a symbol of a Mother Tree with winding hands encircling it. It looked like a mixture of entwined goblin and elven hands.

Alistar opened the book and read:

Dormant days the tree will lay
Until the The Blended finds their ways
Gather the Blade, and pay the cost
To regain the power that has been lost
Follow the Book and what is posed

> *To open the gates that once were closed*
> *The Blended will endure hardship and pain*
> *To forge a path where peace will reign*

He closed the book and began telling Na'lah the history of the elves and the goblins. He told her of a time when the two races were not enemies but allies. The elves were the caretakers of the Mother Trees in the Grove. They looked after them and planted the seeds that fell from the Great Mother Tree. The elves sang and danced for the trees in bright, beautiful ceremonies, whispering magic into the young saplings.

"That's ridiculous. Only goblins have a connection to the Mother Tree."

"So you were taught from birth. There's more," Alistar continued.

The goblins' role was to communicate with the Mother Trees, tapping into the magic the elves had woven into the trees from the time they were seedlings. The goblins also danced and sang around the trees in grand ceremonies, drawing magic from the trees. Goblin Shamanka listened to the spirits of deceased goblins *and* elves and guided those spirits through magical doorways in the Mother Trees into the Halls of the Dead.

"Both goblins and elves? Why would goblin Shamanka guide elves to the Halls of the Dead?"

"Because the two races had to work together. Without the initial magic from the elves, the trees would not grow. Without the goblins, there would be no guides through the Gray Mists into the Halls of the Dead. Now listen, we do not have a lot of time."

He continued.

In addition to serving as guides for the dead, select goblin Shamankas were granted visions and foresight.

"The prophecies!" Na'lah said. "Mother was telling the truth."

"Of course she was. Now, listen!"

On rare occasions, special Shamanka learned to wield magic from the trees.

The Blended.

These were not simply guides for the spirits but living connections between the Mother Trees and all the spirits and magic residing inside. But these Blended were rare in history, manifesting only when the Mother Trees needed them most. Not fully goblin or elf, the Blended took the shape of either species... or both.

Na'lah's jaw went slack. "Both?"

Alistar grinned. "Are things beginning to sound familiar, *Ghost Girl*, with your skin that is too pale for a goblin, eyes too blue, and ears that look, if I may say it without being too rude, like an elf's?"

Na'lah stared into space. "I don't understand. How?"

Alistar held up a hand. "There's more. Listen. Time is short. Records in this book show both of our people have produced a Blended. The last one was an elf who died centuries ago."

"So, there were other Blended?" Na'lah shook her head. "Sounds like a bedtime story."

"This is no tale. There have been many throughout history. The stories say that when one passed from this life, the Mother Tree would manifest a new Blended and the cycle would continue. But a Blended has not been seen for centuries, ever since our people split."

"Manifest? How?"

"No one knows. Sometimes, the child appears in a temple. Other times, a child of power is found in the woods. They are not fully from goblins or elves, but from the Mother Tree itself. Let me continue. We are running short on time. The Elder and Elisara will be coming for you soon. They want war, and you are the perfect symbol to get what they want."

Alistar leaned in closer and continued.

This symbiotic relationship allowed the Blended to see visions, realms, and intentions that others could not. It was said they could communicate with nature itself, bend it to their will, open gates that allowed the dead to pass, and even heal the wounded.

The goblins needed the elves because they could not grow Mother Trees on their own. And the elves needed the goblins' connection to the trees, which allowed them to guide the spirits of the dead into the afterlife. Nature had created a plan for elves and goblins to work and live together in harmony, as they did for many centuries.

But then, Councils of Elders were formed on both sides. Originally, these Elders managed the temples and oversaw the work of the Shamanka. In time, these Elders saw that having control of Ahman'Dur and the Mother

Trees could give them ultimate control over both races. Greed prevailed. And that is when the great war began.

The desire for wealth became a driving force.

The war lasted decades and was only resolved after the elves took control of the Grove and the land around it. The goblins stole mature trees and replanted them in their cities. Both sides thought they were victorious, but in the end, all suffered.

"This cannot be true."

"I know this is a lot to hear, Na'lah," Alistar said. "But this information about the past could put an end to the rivalry between our races. The Blended could help us reconnect to the Mother Trees. We believe you, Na'lah, are the connection we have been looking for. The Blended one."

"You said 'we.' Are there other elves looking for me too?"

"No, Na'lah," Alistar said looking down. "I was working with your father, Torrin. We met some time ago, but that is another story. We were together when we found this book. It opened our eyes to the corruption in both Councils. We saw them for what they were... greedy." Alistar paused, studying Na'lah's face. "We knew if this information got out too soon, your life would be in peril. That's why your father never told anyone... even you. It wasn't until recently, when your father fell ill, that he shared the secret."

"Who would he share the secret with?"

Alistar raised his eyebrows. "I think you know."

Na'lah chewed the inside of her lip. "Garak! Papa told Garak when we went to see him."

"Yes. He sent word through Garak, hoping to get you to Ahman'Dur. Together, we were going to help you bring back the magic."

"Why didn't Papa just tell me?"

Alistar smiled. "If I know Torrin, he wanted you to find your own path. And he was right."

"But if I had known sooner, I could have protected myself from the Council! They tried to set me up!"

"From what Garak told me, it wasn't the whole Council. It was Narlak and his allies."

"But why would Narlak want me to assassinate you?"

"Simple. Think of what Narlak would accomplish had you been successful. I would be dead. You would be caught and executed. With us gone, so too is the possibility of peace between our people. That was why I had to get you out of there today. But my little show on the stage will not stall the Elders for long." Alistar tightened his grip on the book. "Our Councils want war. They profit when innocent blood is spilled."

Suddenly, there was shouting outside the tent. Commands were being shouted. Crates slammed to the ground. The noise was getting closer to the tent with every breath.

"I know this is all a lot to take in, Na'lah, but you must trust me. We must get you out of here. Now. If we want to have any hope for peace, we must continue what your father and I started." Alistar grabbed a knife and cut her bindings. "I can explain more once you are safe. But if we stay here, they will kill both of us, and the chance of peace dies with us."

The voices were dangerously close now.

Na'lah's bonds fell to the floor. She recognized one of the voices all too well. Elisara!

"We must hurry!" Alistar hissed.

A voice from outside the tent shouted, "They're in Alistar's tent! Hurry!"

Elisara.

Na'lah rubbed her wrists. "I don't understand everything you've told me, but I know I don't want to die." She gave Alistar a nod. "Let's go."

15

Together Again

The flap to the tent opened. One of Alistar's guards poked his head inside. "Alistar! Council members are demanding to see the goblin."

Alistar shifted his body in front of Na'lah to hide her from the guard before the soldier's eyes could adjust to the tent's darkened interior. "Hold them off for a bit, my friend. I'm not done questioning her yet."

"Sir?"

"Do you trust me?"

The guard looked back out the tent at the approaching crowd. "You? Yes. Her?"

Alistar held up his hands. "I get it. Just hold them off."

"Sir!" The guard dropped the tent's flap.

Alistar grunted and smirked. "My guards are loyal. They'll keep Elisara and the others busy for a bit, but we don't have long." He hurried to his cot, where the guards

had tossed Na'lah's adventure pack and bow. "Here," Alistar said, handing Na'lah her things.

Na'lah took the pack and looked around. "Wait, my sword!"

Alistar shrugged. "What about it?"

"It's gone! That was my father's sword." She ground her teeth when the realization hit her. "That ranger captain, Elisara, must have taken it when I wasn't looking."

Alistar froze. "Your father's sword?"

"Yes."

"I see. Well, we'll have to deal with that later."

"No, we need to deal with the sword now. I think my father's sword might be important."

Alistar shook his head. "Of course it's important, but we need to go."

He reached beneath his cot to produce an elven shortsword in a finely crafted leather sheath. He tossed the sheathed blade to Na'lah. "Here, use this instead." He dug under the cot a bit more and found another shortsword, this one far older. "We'll see how I fare with one arm." He shrugged the arm in the sling. Then, he stuffed the ancient book into a backpack and, without waiting to see if Na'lah was following, hurried to the far edge of his tent and lifted the oiled canvas. "Let's go!"

Na'lah met Alistar at the back of the tent and ducked outside.

Elf and goblin blinked at the bright sun overhead. Alistar, with his sheathed shortsword in his good hand, tapped Na'lah on the shoulder. "They have us surrounded."

Several pairs of elven guards scurried about, shouting to one another. Alistar scanned the area behind his tent. "Okay. I see how we can do this. Let's get out of here before they realize we left. Follow me!" He ducked under a wagon and crawled away. Na'lah dropped in behind him.

He led them on a wide arc through the village, dipping into shadows beneath the low-hanging awnings of huts, behind several closely packed merchant carts, and through the vegetable gardens sprinkled between buildings. They came to the wall protecting the village. When the guards weren't looking, they slipped over the village wall like passing shadows. They made for the edge of the woods and crouched in the underbrush. "There," Alistar whispered, pointing to a circle of carts.

Na'lah peered across an open field of clover bathed in brilliant sunlight. "What's that?"

"Those carts," Alistar answered with a lift of his chin, "are part of my wagon train. Your brother is there."

Na'lah stiffened. "Badwin? Here?"

"Yes, I wanted to keep an eye on him. I didn't trust my healers to tend him properly if I wasn't present, so I brought him with me."

Na'lah rose to her feet and started for the carts. "Come on! I have to see him!"

Alistar grabbed Na'lah by the scruff of her leather armor and yanked her down with his good arm. "Across an open field? Have you lost your mind?" He gestured to the underbrush surrounding the village. "Better to remain unseen. Come."

Alistar moved with the grace of a jungle cat just inside the brush line. Na'lah admired the smooth flow of his strides and the clean breaks he made between patches of light and shadow. Alistar had been trained and trained well. Something about the way he moved reminded her of Garak. She shrugged and followed closely on his heels.

Soon, the pair found themselves near the dozen or so carts and wagons making up Alistar's caravan. Almost a dozen guards stood about, but their attention was on the center of the village, where shouts and clanging steel announced the continuation of the elves' internal strife. Alistar leaned close to Na'lah. "There," he whispered, pointing at a wagon with a cage made of iron bars. "That's your brother's cart."

Na'lah nodded and checked the guards. When she was certain their attention was on the fighting at the center of the village, she dashed for the far side of Badwin's wheeled cage. Grabbing the bars, she hoisted herself up. "Badwin?" she whispered, and then sucked her breath through her teeth at what she saw.

Her brother lay against the far side of the cage, leaning against the bars. Badwin's face, normally a healthy sheen of gray, was now pale and faintly green. Beads of sweat dabbled his face like glistening diamonds. The flesh of his shoulder blazed red with infection around the festering arrow wound. A bandage, dark with crusted blood, covered the arrow hole in his shoulder. Flies, fat and black, buzzed about the bandage. Green guilt roiled in her gut. This was her fault. She never should have abandoned him. "Badwin?"

Her brother groaned. His head rolled to the side. A line of clear saliva spilled over his chapped lips.

"Blazing Sky Fire," Na'lah quietly cursed. "I'm so sorry."

Alistar came to Na'lah's side. She shot him a frown. "I thought you were taking care of him."

Alistar shrugged. "I never said I was a healer."

"He's almost dead!"

"He's alive. He'd be dead if I had left him behind." Alistar pulled a key out of his pocket and opened the iron cage. "Get your brother while we still can."

Na'lah hopped into the wheeled cell and scurried to her brother. She held him close and tapped his clammy cheek. "Badwin? Can you hear me?"

Badwin struggled to open his heavy lids. His eyes rolled. "Na'lah? Am I dreaming?"

"No, I'm here. Can you stand?"

"Hurry! They're coming!" Alistar hissed from the cage door.

Badwin struggled to stand. His legs, thin beneath his woolen trousers, quivered. Finally, he collapsed against his sister's side. He shook his head. "I'm too weak."

Na'lah scowled at Alistar. "His wound is infected. He's burning with fever."

Alistar rolled his eyes. "I told you, I'm not a healer." He glanced over Na'lah's shoulder. "Hurry! The guards won't be distracted for long!"

Na'lah turned her keen ears toward the center of the village, where the din of elf fighting elf drew closer and closer. She grit her teeth. Alistar was right. If they didn't move quickly, they would have to deal with the whole elven village, not just these few guards. Na'lah slipped her hands under Badwin's armpits to drag him from the cage. But the mere touch of his wounded shoulder brought a cry of pain from his lips. "Sorry!" she breathed.

Several of the guards turned at the sound. When they saw Na'lah in the cage with Badwin, their eyes went wide. Drawing longswords from their sides, they dashed forward. "You there! Stop!"

Na'lah grabbed her brother and tried to pick him up. "Come on, Badwin! We have to go!"

A pair of crows croaked at one another overhead, and suddenly the iron door of the cage clanged shut behind her. Na'lah whirled, and her gut clenched. It was Alistar, his face bent in a grim frown. Na'lah's mind whirled. "Alistar? What?"

But he ignored her and called to the guards instead. "Don't worry. I have them."

The kindness she saw earlier in his face was gone, replaced with a steely cool. He walked over to the guards, who were almost to the caged wagon. "The Elders wanted me to question this hunter after the Council meeting. She'll be coming with us when we leave," he said to the guards. "Sorry to surprise you." As he walked around the cage to intercept the guards, he ran his good hand under the straw covering the floor of the cage. Something scraped over the wood-planked floor.

The guards eyed Na'lah suspiciously. "You transported the prisoner by yourself? With your arm in a sling?"

Alistar laughed. "You think I can't handle a goblin hunter alone? You wound me."

The guard who had spoken returned the laugh. "You are amazing, Alistar, but one of these days, your confidence is going to get you in trouble."

Alistar offered a smug smile. "We'll see about that. Shall we get the wagons ready?"

"As you command."

The guards moved toward the horses, who were tied off to hitching posts at the near side of the clearing. When their backs were turned, Alistar shot Na'lah a quick look, his eyes flashing at the place his hand had slipped under the straw. Confused, Na'lah scrambled on hands and knees across the cage. The key! She clenched it in her fist. So, Alistar hadn't betrayed her after all! Checking on the guards, who were occupied with the horses, Na'lah moved toward the door of the cage, key in hand.

"You!" came a screech like a bolt of lightning across the glade.

Na'lah, fearing she had been caught, spun on her hands and knees to see what this new danger could be. When she saw who had entered the glade, her hopes sagged.

Elisara.

Now she was here.

And she wasn't alone.

Storming across the glade with Elisara was a team of elven rangers, the same ones who had captured Na'lah at the foot of the Mother Tree. Elisara glared at Alistar. "You've messed up for the last time, Alistar. I have my command from the High Council. This ends here."

Alistar held his good hand in the air. "Elisara, what's going on? I just brought the prisoner back to my wagon train. See? She's in the cage."

Elisara didn't bother looking at Na'lah and kept her burning gaze trained on Alistar. "Nice try, traitor. If you were so honest, why did you slip out the back of your tent?"

Alistar shrugged. "Alright, yes. I snuck her out. But the Council wants her dead, and I'm not finished questioning her yet."

Alistar's guardsmen, who had left the horses to stand at their commander's side, put their hands on the hilts of their weapons. "Sir," the one who had spoken earlier said, "what's going on?"

"I'll tell you what's going on," Elisara said with a sneer, "your commander has been playing us for fools.

He's been in league with the goblins to betray the Mother Trees to them."

The guardsmen's shoulders slackened. "Commander?"

"Don't listen to her," Alistar said. "She and the Council have been lying to all of us!"

"Traitor!" Elisara screeched and tore a gleaming shortsword from her side.

Trapped in the cage, Na'lah's heart leapt when she saw the steel in Elisara's deadly grip—her father's sword! "No!" Na'lah yelled, but no one paid any attention to her.

Elisara fell upon Alistar with a blazing flurry of slashes and thrusts, her keen craft a blur of precision. Alistar staggered backwards in a clumsy attempt to dodge the attacks, his sword still in its scabbard. Na'lah gripped the bars of her cage, resisting the urge to leap out and fight by Alistar's side. *No*, she told herself, *I need to get Badwin out of here.* "This is going to hurt," she whispered to her brother. "Be strong." Grabbing Badwin by the armpits, she dragged him across the cage while watching the sword fight in the glade. Badwin moaned but didn't cry out.

Alistar's guardsmen had their steel out, parrying the whirlwind that was Elisara's maddened attack, giving their commander the moment he needed to draw his own weapon with his good hand. But the loyalty to their commander came at a price. Elisara, in her rage, cut down first one, and then another of Alistar's personal guardsmen. They fell, groaning, to their knees, hot blood watering the thirsty soil.

"No!" Alistar screamed, and leapt forward to stand over his wounded guards. His shortsword flashed in the sunlight and clanged against the keen metal of Papa's blade.

Na'lah grit her teeth. She dumped Badwin by the cage's door and fumbled for the key Alistar had given her. Her hands shook, and she dropped the key twice. "Blazing Sky Fires!" she muttered. "Get ahold of yourself!" Somehow, Na'lah snatched up the key and jammed it in the keyhole. She turned until she heard a sharp click. The door swung open. "Come on," she whispered to her brother, and pulled him from the caged wagon and onto the ground, where they fell in a tangled lump on the far side of the wagon.

The crack of metal and a cry from the glade sounded over the clash of arms. Na'lah risked a look to find Alistar holding the hilt of his shattered shortsword before him like a useless toy. The broken upper half of his sword lay sparkling in the grass at his feet. Elisara and her few encircling rangers closed their ring on him one step at a time. The elven ranger cackled. "And to think," Elisara growled, "that I once worshiped the ground you walked on." She raised Na'lah's father's blade in the air, where it flashed in the sunlight. "Never again!" Elisara came at him then, Alistar's doom riding upon a sunbeam.

Na'lah pushed herself to her feet, ready to dash across the glade. Wounded brother or no, she could not watch her new ally stand unarmed against impossible odds. She tore the elven shortsword from her belt and took a step toward the fight. Suddenly, the sharp twang of short bows filled the glade with zipping ash shafts. The arrows *thunked* into Elisara's unsuspecting rangers. Two of her closest fellows dropped to their knees, clutching at the feathered shafts sprouting from their chests. Elisara, Alistar, Na'lah, and every eye in the glade cast their glances about, straining to find the source of this newest wave of attacks.

They didn't have long to wait.

The underbrush exploded in an emerald cloud of leaves as Garak and Skronk burst into the sunlight, their keen blades bared and ready. Elisara's eyes went wide. "Goblins!" she screamed. "Alistar's allies! Kill them!"

Elisara's remaining rangers charged their hated enemies. The long-time foes came together with a resounding crash, filling the glade with the ringing of steel and cries of the wounded. Elisara leveled her shortsword at Alistar's throat. "Enough playing around. Now you die, goblin-friend!"

Across the glade, Garak drove his blade through his opponent's chest and kicked the body to the ground. He picked up the dead elf's sword and tossed it hilt first to Alistar. "Catch!"

Alistar leapt from the ring of guards and caught the tossed weapon. He whirled the blade before him and dropped into a fighting crouch.

Na'lah snapped out of the surprise of seeing her brother and Skronk. She charged into the sunlight, waving her sword. "Elisara!" she screamed. "You're mine!"

Garak parried the attacks of two elves, disarming one and opening the throat of another. "No!" he barked at Na'lah. "She is mine!" He jerked a thumb at the tree line. "Get Badwin out of here!"

Na'lah skidded to a stop. "No! I won't leave you!"

Garak turned his back on his younger sister and faced Elisara just as another dozen elven rangers poured into the glade. "Na'lah!" Garak barked. "Get Badwin and finish the mission!"

The hunter in her screamed for her bow, yammered for the fight. How could she leave her brother and allies when they needed her most? Isn't leaving an ally behind exactly how all of this started? Na'lah couldn't let them sacrifice themselves for her. That's not how it was supposed to work.

She screamed in frustration, drawing the attention of several of the elven rangers, who pulled up on their battle charge to yank short bows from their shoulders. Rage beat like a bitter drum in Na'lah's veins. The pounding in her head silenced even the cries of the dying. Na'lah dropped to her knees and punched the ground in frustration. She crammed her fingertips into the sandy soil, bending back her nails until they broke. "No!" she screamed, clutching the soil as the first round of elven arrows took flight, a chaotic chorus of hissing death.

Then, the ground beneath her quivered, just like it had at the Mother Tree. The earth wriggled and rippled across the glade, springing up like thin strips of kelp wavering in the sea. Roots, some thin, some thick, erupted from the ground and caught the arrows mid-flight.

Elisara's troops fell away from the barrier with cries of fear. Garak grabbed hold of Alistar and dragged him and one of Alistar's surviving guards towards the woods. The rest of Alistar's personal guard, a good half dozen, formed a wedge behind their leader and followed him into the woods. Na'lah looked at the writhing roots that had appeared out of nowhere and then at her hands. "What is happening?"

Suddenly, there was someone at her side, shaking her. She turned, dumbly, and found it was Klier. "Klier? What are you doing here?"

"No time to chat," he huffed. "We need to go. Now."

16

Choose Your Own Adventure

N a'lah felt the Mother Trees before she could see them, a pulsing in her veins. Familiar, like a heartbeat, a thousand ants racing back and forth across her limbs. Not enough to bother her, but strong enough to sense. The tingling grew with every step. When she stepped through the thicket of the forest and into Ahman'Dur, the feeling exploded and was suddenly gone.

Na'lah, Badwin, and Klier stumbled towards the largest Mother Tree in the center of the grove. As they drew closer, Na'lah pulled back and dropped Badwin's arm. He collapsed in a lump at her feet.

"I'm not going near that thing," she said, pointing to the massive tree dominating the grove. "The last time I was here, it swallowed Hobler."

Klier looked up at the Mother Tree. "Garak said we had to get you both to the tree. We don't have time to

question him." Without waiting for her response, Klier dragged Badwin toward the base of the tree by himself while Na'lah stood staring at the massive trunk.

Klier set Badwin's back against the tree and then rummaged through his pack and pulled out a pouch of yarrow. In no time at all, Klier had new bandages over Badwin's infected shoulder. Once he was finished, he came back to Na'lah, who was still staring up at the Mother Tree. Klier pointed at Badwin, slumped against the tree trunk. "He needs medicine, and he needs it fast!"

Na'lah stared at the tree. Klier waved his hand in front of Na'lah's face. "Na'lah, did you hear me? Badwin will die if we don't do something!" He grabbed her shoulders and shook her.

Na'lah's mind spun until she heard a loud crash from the woods. Na'lah and Klier drew their weapons. They crept back to Badwin, forming a protective shield around him while never taking their eyes off the tree line. Na'lah returned her short sword to its sheath and grabbed her bow from her back while nocking an arrow. *I may be missing some fingers, but I'll pick off enough to make them think twice.*

The noises grew louder. Na'lah pulled back on the bow, wincing from her missing fingers. She held steady, ready to take out the first elf through the brush. She saw movement, branches and leaves shivering, and took aim. An arm crashed through. Na'lah let fly. At that moment, someone screamed, "Na'lah!"

Something broke through the forest at a full sprint, and Na'lah jerked instinctively. The bow caught a small portion of the arrow's nock and pitched it to the side.

Garak froze as the arrow headed towards him. With no time to drop, the arrow went straight through the tip of his right ear. "Blazing Sky Fires, that was close!" Garak put his hand to his ear, feeling for damage. The arrow lodged into one of the trees behind him and quivered from the impact. "Save your arrows for the elves, you stupid *warrok*. You will need them if your aim is that poor." He touched his ear. His fingertips came away glistening red. Garak marched toward Na'lah and Klier near the Mother Tree. He looked past them, to the lump next to the tree, and pulled up. He frowned, his eyes dark. "What in the Blazing Sun are you doing? Heal him before he dies. What's wrong with you?"

"I don't know how. I've never..."

"You're the Blended, or so our old man says. Figure it out, Na'lah. I didn't spend time in the Iron Box saving you for nothing."

"The last time I tried, the tree took Hobler. I'm not the Blended."

"Our old man says you are," Garak spat. He grabbed her tunic and yanked her towards him. "Supposedly some book foretold it."

There was another crash near the edge of the forest. The group turned to see Alistar, Skronk, and the last of Alistar's guards emerging, almost a dozen in all. Bursting from the tree line, they made straight for the Mother

Tree. All were haggard, covered in crusted blood and dirt. Alistar still had a sword in hand.

The underbrush rustled again. Elisara and her rangers charged into the glade, Elisara brandishing Torrin's sword. They were only a few steps behind Alistar, twenty rangers bent on revenge. A few more steps, and they would reach Na'lah and her group.

Garak turned to Klier. "Get ready. We're in for another scuffle."

Na'lah put her bow on her back and pulled out her shortsword. "If we are going out, brother, let's take a lot of them with us." She spread her arms wide and crouched like a panther.

"'We?' We are not going to do anything. You are going to figure out your connection to the Mother Tree while we buy you a few more breaths." And with that, he shoved her toward the Mother Tree.

Na'lah stumbled, arms flailing for balance. Right when she thought she had it, her last step found Badwin's sprawled leg. Na'lah tumbled backwards in slow motion.

Right at the Mother Tree.

Eyes wide.

Mouth open.

Arms extended to protect her fall.

Bracing for impact.

Hands finding the trunk.

An enormous boom thundered from the Mother Tree. A shockwave pulsed and traveled outwards.

Na'lah flew and landed hard on the ground. She got to her hands and knees. Dazed, she shook her head and looked around. Her eyes bulged as she took in the scene. A crow frozen in mid-flight. Garak pulling another knife from its sheath. Klier stuck in mid-motion, nocking an arrow. Alistar in mid-stride, reaching for the Mother Tree, Skronk right behind him. And farther past them, a group of elven rangers with Elisara at the lead, Na'lah's father's sword glinting in the afternoon sun.

Frozen.

All frozen in place.

Na'lah slowly rose to her feet. She scanned the surroundings again, not believing what she was seeing. Not a branch moved. Not a leaf swayed. Even the dust cloud under Alistar's foot was frozen in mid-air. It was as if time had just stopped. Nothing moved. No one collapsed.

They were just... frozen.

In place.

A hum pierced the silence. It was quiet at first, but it grew in intensity. Na'lah turned around, looking for the source. The humming grew louder and louder. She turned toward the massive Mother Tree. Yes, that was it. The source of the humming. When the humming reached its apex, and the vibrations were pulsing rapidly, everything stopped. The humming. The vibrations. Gone.

And out of the Mother Tree's trunk stepped a Spirit Walker, straight through the bark. It stepped into the light, revealing a lowered cowl. Na'lah gasped as she recognized the Spirit Walker wearing her face. "You!" she spat. "What do you want?"

"Huntress... the time has come," the Spirit Walker hissed and advanced towards her. Its face melted and shifted before Na'lah's eyes and took the form of something ancient. Its face was round with long ears that pointed up and back like antennas. Black, swirling pools stared straight at Na'lah. Leathery skin hung from its wrists and folded upon itself in places. Strands of black, gnarled hair dripped in patches over its temples and draped over the robe. It spasmed and hunched over until it crouched on all fours.

It pointed a crooked finger at Na'lah. "I warned you that your closed heart and fixed mind would have consequences. You chose the path of the warrior, where you should have heeded the call of the Spirits. You neglected them, and in doing so, you have damned others to perish. A price needs to be paid for your ignorance."

"A price for what, Walker? What ignorance? Stop with your riddles. I can fix whatever you throw at me."

The Spirit Walker swayed back and forth on its haunches. A guttural laugh slipped out. "The arrogance, child. The very flaw that put all of this into motion many, many years ago. Thinking of yourself and not the whole is what destroyed the balance. You were meant to restore balance, but you still have not learned. No, no...

you still have not learned. Perhaps you are not strong enough yet," it wheezed, shaking its head.

"Try me, Spirit. I have overcome obstacles, trials, and tribulations. I can overcome whatever you place before me." Na'lah lifted her chin in defiance.

"Ahh..." the Spirit mocked. "Strength, yes, strength. This will take strength to complete. But it is not the type of strength you yet possess, huntress."

The Spirit Walker straightened from its crouch. It glided towards Na'lah. She reached for her shortsword, only to find it was not there.

"There is no need for such things here, huntress," the Walker said as it circled Na'lah. "That is not the strength you will need to restore balance." The creature stopped behind her and put its gnarled hand on her shoulder.

A shiver ran down Na'lah's back.

One finger rose to point, and Na'lah's head turned to follow. She let out a gasp as roots from the Mother Tree wrapped around Badwin. They ensnared him until his body disappeared beneath the twisted bark of wriggling roots. The tree shivered, and then bit by bit, the roots dragged Badwin underground.

"No! Not again!" Na'lah lunged for Badwin, but the Spirit Walker's grip was a vice holding her in place.

"Strength. Yes, strength it will take to restore the power that was lost, Na'lah. The Spirits demand it. Neglect. Many, many years of neglect." The Walker's cold breath lay heavy on Na'lah's neck. Gooseflesh rose along her spine. The Spirit Walker chuckled. "But do you have the strength to make the right choices for goblins *and* elves? To bring back balance? Or will your arrogant, fixed mind and closed heart be the downfall of all?"

Na'lah stared at the spot where Badwin disappeared. Her heart sank, and her shoulders drooped in defeat. *This cannot be happening. How do I fight this? Am I truly lost?* "Tell me what I have to do, Walker." Na'lah's voice trembled. Her vision blurred with wetness. "Enough riddles."

"To restore balance, you must have balance inside you. Come to peace with who you are. Hobler suffered a dagger because he loved you, and yet you shut him out... closed heart." The spirit hissed and pointed a bony finger at the Mother Tree.

The ground shook.

The earth parted, and a hole opened.

Roots rose, lifting Hobler's body from its cold crypt. Even from this distance, Na'lah could see him softly breathing, engulfed by the Mother Tree's roots.

"And your dear brother took an arrow, protecting you from the elves. Did you really think you alone could stop a war? Arrogant, and yet, not so far from the truth of the matter..." The Walker wiggled a finger.

The Mother Tree groaned in response, and the roots reached for the sky. Both Badwin and Hobler rose into the air, their chests rising and falling weakly.

"You may use the power that resides in you to heal one or both. But be warned, if you choose to heal both, your ability to heal will not be restored and the Mother

Trees will once again become dormant until another Blended is born. Or you can honor your brother and friend's decisions to protect you and let one of them move on to become one with the Mother Tree." The Spirit Walker circled Na'lah until it was between her and the Mother Tree. "What will the famed huntress choose?"

"Why me? Why is this happening to me, you foul creature?" Na'lah stared into those black swirling holes.

"Ahhh... the third and final reason. You are not of one path, Na'lah. You walk two paths in this world. But your mind is so fixed that blindness overcomes you at every step. When you find balance, you will find freedom. And being free, you will see more than you can ever imagine."

The Walker bent even closer until its grim, gray lips almost touched Na'lah's ear. "Now choose."

17

A Legend Is Born

Na'lah tightened her fist. White pain flared in the flesh where her shooting fingers used to be. She scowled at the Spirit Walker. "You want me to choose between saving Badwin and Hobler or giving up this path I don't want to walk?" The hunter spit at the Spirit Walker's feet. "That's no choice at all. To the Pit with your spirit world and everything to do with it. I choose my friends and family."

The Spirit Walker's lips split in a cold crease, revealing white canines and bleeding gums. "So arrogant. You have much to learn." The creature drew a ghastly hand across its gray face, and a distorted version of Na'lah's own face reappeared. "And so little time to learn it."

A chill breeze crept through the grove. The Mother Tree's leaves frowned and rustled, turning their silver bellies away from Na'lah's defiance. As the breeze left the sacred ground, life clicked once, twice, and then crackled into action.

"You!" Elisara screamed. The elven captain, wielding Na'lah's father's sword, bared her teeth. She locked her deadly gaze upon Na'lah and stormed across the glade. "You will die for your heresy!"

Na'lah jumped back. A cool breeze from the Mother Tree whispered, and Na'lah found her elven sword back in her hands. "What?" she muttered, but this was not time for questions. She twirled her shortsword and made for Elisara. "We'll see about that!"

They came together with a crash at the foot of the Mother Tree just below Hobler and Badwin, who were still suspended in their root-bound crypts, well above the fight. Dappled sunlight glinted off the warriors' ringing blades as the sword masters danced their deadly dance. Elisara's almond eyes flashed behind her scowling visage. "What happened to killing Alistar?" She let fly with a vicious swipe at Na'lah's neck. Na'lah danced out of range, and Elisara growled. "I gave you a simple mission and you couldn't even do that." The captain unleashed a torrent of slashes and thrusts, rattling Na'lah's sword in her weakening grip.

Back and forth across the grove, the sword masters fought as Elisara's unit of elite elven rangers battled the unexpected allies of Garak, Alistar, and his loyal followers. Clanging steel and hoarse battle cries filled the valley of Ahman'Dur. Elven and goblin blood

sprinkled the sacred ground like rain. The watching trees shivered and wept.

Na'lah pressed her attack on Elisara, working first far and then close, dealing damage with fist, elbow, knee, and steel. She caught the elven captain with a delicious double thrust and delivered stinging gashes to Elisara's forearm and thigh. The captain fell back, opening a gap under her arm. Na'lah saw the opening and pressed her advantage, but movement in the surrounding undergrowth caught her attention.

Thin fingers of gray mist crept from the shadows of the surrounding trees. Then, dozens of figures clad in tattered black cloaks drifted forward until the entire grove of Mother Trees were ringed with ghostly specters. Na'lah gasped and pulled back her advantage over Elisara. "Do you see that? What is happening?"

Elisara sneered. "You think I'm a fool? I'm not taking my eyes off you."

"No! Look! Spirits!"

And as she said it, the creatures of the shadow realm drew back their cowls. When she saw their features, Na'lah gasped. "Goblins *and* elves!"

"What are you talking about?"

Na'lah pointed with the tip of her sword, the truth of the matter suddenly clear. "Don't you see the ghosts of the dead? Elves and goblins both! Our dead are trapped in The Gray Mists. They can't move on to the Halls of the Dead without the Mother Trees! It's real," she

whispered, thinking of Mother and Papa. "They were right all along."

Elisara shot a quick glance at her sides. "I see nothing, assassin. Nothing but your doom!" Elisara screamed and drove Na'lah back with a storm of slashes and thrusts, driven by a fury only the truly fanatic can muster.

Step by step, the elven captain pushed Na'lah backwards until Na'lah was pinned against a copse of young Mother Trees. Seeing her advantage, Elisara feinted a high strike at Na'lah's head. As soon as Na'lah raised her blade to defend against the attack, Elisara changed direction and slashed at Na'lah's unprotected belly. Thanks to her years of training with Master Goggins, Na'lah recognized the ploy. She dropped an elbow to close off her vulnerable ribs, but it was too late. Elisara pressed the edge of Torrin's blade against Na'lah's unprotected belly and tore across the exposed flesh. "Die!"

But Na'lah of Draal was not one to give in so easily.

She clamped her elbow down, pinning Elisara's sword and stopping the attack before it liberated the gray snakes of her intestines. Na'lah's head swooned. A wave of nausea rippled through her, bringing the taste of green, green bile to her tongue. She grit her teeth and grabbed the hilt of her father's sword, now wedged deeply in the thin meat and bones of her lower ribs. Elisara yanked at the weapon, but Na'lah would not

relent. "Let go!" the elven captain hissed. "And let me finish this, you freak of nature!"

Na'lah dropped her weight and pulled Elisara off balance. The two came together, their heads smacking one another until Na'lah's eyes flashed white with pain. Na'lah dropped her gaze as she wrestled with Elisara, her eyes falling upon the polished steel of her father's sword. The blade glimmered. *Is that the sun? No, we're in the Mother Tree's shade.* Her head swooned, and she looked closer.

At first, Na'lah saw the expected gray and white flashings of Elisara and Na'lah's bare arms as they grappled for the now glowing weapon. But the images in her father's blade wavered, and suddenly Na'lah saw, as clearly as though she were there, the inside of her parents' hut.

Her mother was crying at the side of Papa's bed. "Torrin!" Na'lah heard her mother call. "Don't leave me!" Na'lah watched her mother, who, despite her words, drew her father's blanket over his head, and then collapsed, sobbing, on the cold chest of the goblin she loved.

The taste of metal filled Na'lah's mouth. This was no ordinary vision in her father's blade. Something from deep inside told Na'lah that what she had seen was real.

Her father was dead.

"Papa!" Na'lah's limbs went slack. Her father, her anchor, was dead. Na'lah rode another wave of nausea.

"What's the point?" she muttered, and let loose her hold on the sword.

Elisara shouted and stepped away, tearing Torrin's blade from Na'lah's side. The elven captain regarded Na'lah with a sneer. "I don't know what you're babbling about, and I don't care. Today, you die, and the war begins!" She raised Torrin's sword over her head, ready to finish the fight.

Suddenly, from the side, two lithe forms careened into Elisara and tackled her to the ground. Na'lah, clutching her butchered ribs, watched Alistar and Garak wrestle Elisara for control of the clearly glowing sword. *Why is the sword glowing?* Garak got a lock on Elisara's sword arm and delivered a brutal elbow to the elven captain's jaw. Elisara groaned and spit blood. Her eyes rolled back in her head. She let slip her grasp on Torrin's sword. Garak wrenched their father's blade free of Elisara's control and tossed it to Na'lah. It thumped on the mossy forest floor. Garak cranked Elisara's arm behind her back. She rolled with the movement and kneed Garak in the groin. He grunted through gritted teeth but kept his hold on the mighty elven captain. "Take the sword!" he barked. "Do what you need to do!"

Still clutching her battered side, Na'lah crawled to the sword and picked it up. Her father's blade buzzed in her grip, filling her with newfound vigor. Na'lah's eyes cleared, and she looked around the Mother Tree grove.

More spirits of the dead drifted from the shadows, filling the glade to the point where Na'lah could no longer see the underbrush behind them. Whenever she met their eyes, the phantoms would incline their heads toward the great Mother Tree behind her. Finally, slowly, hesitantly, Na'lah turned and looked upon the sacred tree.

A low hum radiated from its trunk and filled the air with a golden glow. Na'lah dropped her gaze to the blade. *The buzzing in the sword and the tree... they're the same.* Her eyes settled on the weapon, a quiet knowing filled her being. "I know what I have to do," she muttered. "But..."

"Then do it, you stupid *warrok*!" Garak barked, trying to tear his forearm from Elisara's teeth. "We are risking our lives for you!"

Na'lah shook her head. "I can't. I'm not... I'm not a priestess. That's not who I am."

"Na'lah, please!" Alistar begged, trying to get ahold of Elisara with his one, good arm and getting a fist to the jaw as his reward. "This is bigger than you. Your people need you! Our people need you!"

The fighting raged around her. Goblins screamed. Elves fell. But in the chaos of it all, Na'lah felt thick and slow, as though she were underwater, unable to move, to think. Elisara freed an elbow and slammed Garak's belly. He coughed and used an armbar to flip Elisara over and pin her to the ground. "Na'lah! Now!"

Na'lah shook her head again. Gripping her father's sword, she staggered to her feet. "No. I am a hunter. It's who I was meant to be. Find someone else to be your chosen oracle. My path lies elsewhere." She looked at Hobler and Badwin, still suspended in the air by the Mother Tree's writhing roots. "And besides, it's the only way to bring both of them back."

"Blazing Sky Fires, you stupid *warrok*! Why do you think they died for you?"

"They're not dead yet. Not if I can save them."

Garak growled with rage. "Na'lah!"

Na'lah turned her face from her brother and took on the gathered elven and goblin spirits. "Find someone else to guide you to the other side," she said to the ghastly gathering. "I choose life for my brother and Hobler."

The wraiths received Na'lah's words with the grim, gray faces of the dead, accepting her choice that would doom them to an eternity of walking in the Gray Mists. Then, those directly across the glade from Na'lah parted, forming a path. A solitary shadow glided through the low mist until it stood at the forefront of the unearthly creatures. Pale, gray hands rose to the edge of its hood. In one swift motion, it threw back the covering and revealed its identity.

"Papa!" Na'lah cried.

Torrin's calm eyes fell upon his living daughter, and in that instant, Na'lah understood another truth: if she did not open the gate to the afterlife for the tortured souls of the deceased, her father, now a phantom himself, would be condemned to an eternity in the shadowy world between life and death. A gasp slipped from Na'lah's lips. "Papa! No!"

Her father's shade simply closed his eyes and dipped his chin, affirming the fate awaiting him.

"No, no, no!" Na'lah clutched her father's sword and held it before her. She whirled on the Spirit Walker that wore her face, standing at the foot of the great Mother Tree. "Why are you doing this to me? You sick *warrok*! Why are you making me choose?"

The Spirit Walker wearing Na'lah's face glared at her from under a heavy brow. "We are not making you choose. We are making you *see* who you truly are."

Na'lah growled. Fury rattled her spine and clouded her vision. "No! You're taking away everything I ever loved and for what? To help people I never cared about?" And even as the words left her mouth, she remembered her father's shade standing behind her. Her gut clenched, and a sob burst from her lips. She turned to her beloved father. "Papa, I'm sorry. I can't. I just can't."

Torrin's ghost, a light smile upon his lips, nodded in understanding. And without a spoken word from her father, Na'lah knew what he was saying. *The choice is yours. No matter your decision, I will still love you.*

Na'lah's chin trembled. How could one goblin love her so unconditionally? And more, how could Na'lah, in her selfishness, deny her father the long rest he so rightly deserved?

The sword buzzed and glowed in her hands, mimicking the Mother Tree's call. Na'lah knew what she needed to do, even though she did not want to do it. Tears gathered in her eyes, tears for the path of the hunter she was giving up to save her father's soul. She flipped the blade so that it was pointing down. Grasping the hilt with both hands, she drove the polished steel deep into the soil. The blade punched through the soil and pierced a root from the Mother Tree. Something white, something like lightning, shot through Na'lah, and she stood stock still.

Na'lah and the Mother Tree were one.

A deep rumble, distant thunder rolling closer and closer before a storm, barreled through the valley. Overhead in the canopy, a chorus of crows croaked and cackled. The sky darkened, and a chill breeze hissed through the trees. *Listen! Listen! Listen!* Keeping one hand on the hilt of her father's buzzing sword, Na'lah reached with her mangled free hand back toward the great Mother Tree. When she spoke, it was with the voice of something greater than Na'lah the Hunter. Something greater than Na'lah the Shamanka. It was the voice of Great Nature itself. "Spirits of the damned, I, Na'lah of Draal, beckon you forward to pass through the sacred gate. Your time in The Gray Mists has come to an end. Come forward now and pass into the Great Rest that awaits you all."

A great cracking sounded from the grove. All fighting stopped as the combatants froze in stunned confusion to stare at the Mother Tree, where the gnarled bark split at the seams, revealing a yawning gateway to an empty passage beyond.

"The Hall of the Dead," Alistar whispered.

Garak let loose his arm bar on Elisara. "As foretold."

"Look!" cried Klier, pointing to the circle of ghosts in the glade.

Elf and goblin alike shivered as they saw for the first time the gathered assembly of the dead.

Dark storm clouds tumbled overhead, flashing white spears of lightning. The shades drifted forward, and as they did, the onlooking elves and goblins stumbled from their path. "What devilry is this?" Elisara whispered, pushing free of Garak. Her gaze fell upon one phantom in particular. "My dead uncle. Mishintar. But how?"

The elven ghost nodded at Elisara's words and strode forward. Coming to Na'lah, the shadowy elven spirit touched his fingertips to his forehead and bowed low. Then, giving a soft smile to Elisara, the elven spirit passed through the rent in the Mother Tree's trunk and led the procession of the deceased into the afterlife.

Elisara watched them go, goblin and elf, side by side. "What is this?"

Alistar came to stand next to Elisara. He put his good hand on her shoulder. She did not pull away. "It is as we said," he said. "Goblins and elves were not always enemies. We have been lied to."

Elisara shook her head slowly. "How could I have been so wrong?"

Alistar took a slow breath. "We were *all* wrong for too long. But it's up to us to set things on the right path again."

Na'lah's head spun. She tried to watch Alistar and Elisara, but the buzzing sword and the magic passing through her demanded too much attention. Something was coming out of the earth, through the sword, through Na'lah, back through the Mother Tree, and round and round again, in a never-ending cycle. As much as she felt like she was connected to the wild as a hunter, this was something altogether different. With this, Na'lah wasn't connected to the wild.

She was the wild.

This was where she was meant to be. She could be both hunter *and* priestess. Her choice was not a subtraction from who she was, but an addition to who she could be.

As the last of the spirits passed through the gate in the Mother Tree, Na'lah felt a presence at her side. Without looking, she knew who it was.

"Papa."

If he could respond, he said no word. Instead, her father's shade bowed low, touching his fingertips to his forehead. When he stood tall, his eyes beamed with pride and love. Na'lah's chin trembled again. "Goodbye," she whispered. Papa gave her a final nod and drifted to the Mother Tree. He stood in the opening and then turned and waved to Na'lah. Na'lah closed her eyes and sighed. "Goodbye," she whispered again.

Then came the voice of the final Spirit Walker. "It is time to choose, Na'lah of the Short Bow. Badwin or Hobler?"

After grieving the loss of her father, being reminded of the Spirit Walker's choice was like a slap to the face. "Choice?" she muttered. "What more can you take from me that you haven't already taken?" She let out a sigh. "I cannot choose between them."

The Spirit Walker with Na'lah's face smiled, but this time, there was no edge to its words. "Your mind may not be able to choose, but your heart has chosen for you."

As the creature of the shadow realm said the words, the roots holding Hobler dropped him to the ground, where he fell, gasping and coughing. He looked up. "Na'lah?"

But Na'lah's eyes were only for her brother, Badwin, whose battered body suddenly went limp in its rootbound crypt. "Badwin!" Na'lah cried.

Just then, another shade stepped into the glen, its hood thrown back.

"Badwin," Na'lah gasped, looking upon her brother's ghost. "No, no, no!"

Badwin's shade crossed the glen and came to stand beside their father in the hollow of the Mother Tree's belly. Raising their hands, Papa and Badwin waved once and then turned to enter the Halls of the Dead together. They disappeared into the mist, and the opening in the Mother Tree closed like thick curtains over them.

A silence fell upon Ahman'Dur.

Na'lah collapsed to the ground, clutching her wounded side. As much as her belly throbbed from Elisara's slash, the pain in her heart, of losing both her father and brother, cut deeper. She sobbed and sobbed, grief sinking its teeth into her soul.

Garak and Klier were at her side in an instant, cleaning and bandaging her with practiced hands. "We got you," Klier whispered as he worked. "You're going to be fine."

She opened her eyes to find Garak staring at her, his eyes wet and red. "It hurts, doesn't it?"

Na'lah nodded, knowing he wasn't talking about the sword cut.

Garak cleared his throat and looked at the Great Mother, now towering still and silent above them. "Well, it was the right choice," he said, putting a gentle hand on her shoulder. "Looks like you finally got something right."

18

Oh, So That's How It Started

They gathered on a cliff overlooking Ahman'Dur. Alistar had led them there after the final elven and goblin spirits had passed through the Mother Tree and into the Halls of the Dead. "We need to move," he had told them while they were still in the grove. "The Council of Elders will send more soldiers shortly. They'll be in no mood to listen to stories of what we have seen. Not yet, anyway. Come, follow me. There is much to discuss."

It was a short march, not nearly long enough for Na'lah to mull over everything that had happened.

Papa?

Gone.

Badwin?

Gone.

The Mother Tree?

Awake.

The elves?

Allies.

And how could she even begin to explain what was happening with the Mother Tree? The young goblin in her wanted to run to her parents for answers, but Papa was dead. And Mother? Oh, Na'lah could only imagine how she would react to hearing that Badwin was gone.

Gone?

Dead.

Na'lah's chest seized. Her breathing turned to panting. Her chin quivered and before she could stop it, sorrow burst from her throat like a badger from its den. She wept long and loud for her brother, for her father, for the world she knew that was coming apart.

Life had never been easy for Na'lah. Not as Draal's Ghost Girl. No playmates. Few friends. Always the tagalong. It was all she could do to scratch out an existence with Badwin and Papa's support. And now, even this meager life that she had clung to had been ripped away. All that was left of her family was Mother and Garak, each scratchier than the other. She turned and looked for her brother. He was marching behind her, whispering to Alistar. He looked up and caught Na'lah watching him. He lifted his chin in, what was that? Encouragement? Na'lah turned back to the march and shook her head. She must be seeing things in her grief.

She had so many questions. How did Alistar know to look for her? How did he know Papa? What were they going to do now?

Whom could she trust?

Someone came up to march at her side. Hobler. She wiped the tears and snot from her face. "Hey."

"Hey."

They marched for a bit.

When the sorrow grabbed her gut and the tears came, Hobler reached out and touched her hand, but she pulled away. "No. Not yet."

Hobler nodded.

They marched some more. Hobler cleared his throat. "I, uh, I wanted to say, 'Thank you.'"

"Thank you?"

"Yeah. Klier told me what you did."

Na'lah snorted. "I didn't do anything."

"He said you chose me over," he paused, his face twisting in pain, "you know."

Na'lah shook her head. "I didn't do anything," she repeated. "The Mother Tree chose. Not me."

Hobler nodded, his mouth a tight line. "Well, thanks anyway." Then, "I'm here for you. You know that, right?"

Na'lah grunted and patted his arm. She picked up her pace, needing to be alone.

Hobler occupied a special place in her heart. The Mother Tree got that right anyway. But with everything she had lost, she wasn't ready for him to be back in her world. Not yet. She climbed and climbed, letting the rhythm of the quick pace soothe her aching soul.

Alistar, with Garak and Elisara at his side, led the witnesses of what had happened to a secret pass leading out of Ahman'Dur, the Valley of Mother Trees. Once they reached the valley's rim, Alistar assembled the still-stunned goblins and elves. They looked across the valley to the great Mother Tree, her arms stretched protectively over her grove.

Na'lah found herself next to Elisara, who, only a short while ago, was tearing Papa's sword through her belly. Elisara's eyes were glazed and unfocused. Her mouth hung slightly open. She looked at Alistar. "Why hide this from us?"

Na'lah put her hand on Papa's sword, hanging from her belt. The hilt tingled under her grip as if something that had long been asleep was awakening. "Good question," she said. "If you knew the truth, why hide it? So many have died. And the spirits of the dead... trapped in the Gray Mist this whole time."

Alistar sighed. "That's a long story."

"We're not going anywhere," Na'lah snorted.

Elves and goblins shuffled closer. Garak and Hobler stepped to Na'lah's side. Hobler inspected the blade of an elven sword he had picked up after the fight. "Better make it quick. They will be tracking us the first chance they get."

Alistar turned so his back was to the valley. He faced the gathered elves and goblins. "It started when I met Na'lah's father, Torrin."

Na'lah nodded. "You said something about that in your tent. How did you meet?"

"Several years ago, the elven Council of Elders charged me with protecting Ahman'Dur, the sacred grove of Mother Trees." He opened his arms wide to indicate the valley behind him. "I was on patrol when I stumbled on fresh tracks, a goblin hunter. It was just some scuffed moss, but his scent was still in the air. My plan was to put an arrow in him before he knew I was there."

Na'lah frowned. "No one could surprise Papa in the woods."

Alistar grunted. "I learned that the hard way. I was nose down in his tracks when he circled back and jumped me. It was dumb luck that I got my blade out in time. We fought, and he gave me a little reminder for my efforts." The elven leader rolled up the sleeve on his wounded arm and revealed a purple scar running from wrist to elbow. "I was lucky to escape."

Garak dismissed the scar with a wave. "The point?"

Alistar offered an apologetic dip of the head. "Torrin was the better swordsman. We both knew it, but I knew the terrain. This was my territory, after all. I broke away the first chance I got, knowing he would follow me. I led him away from Ahman'Dur, deep into another valley.

"He chased me into a gorge, the steep walls pinching closer and closer. I've always been quick at climbing, but with a wounded arm?" Alistar shook his head. "I would have to turn and fight when the trail ended.

"And that's when I saw it: an archway of carved stone buried beneath a thick blanket of vines and littered leaves. How had I never seen it before? It was my only hope. If I could just lure him into tighter quarters, I could protect my weak side and maybe escape with my life."

Garak crossed his arms over his lean chest. "*This* is a short story?"

Na'lah scowled. "Quiet."

Alistar held up a hand. "Point taken. I'm doing my best." He cleared his throat. "I jumped through the opening and ran into a dark tunnel. At first, I couldn't see a thing. Torrin was right on my tail, taunting me to turn and face him.

"Suddenly, the tunnel opened into a wide cavern filled with sun-starved trees and vines. Weak sunlight filtered through openings in the ceiling, revealing walls carved with half-statues and figurines. I didn't have time to enjoy the artwork, however. Torrin burst into the room and came at me, all blades and teeth, knees and elbows. We battled across the cavern's floor, stumbling over vines and fallen rock in the dim light.

"It was Torrin who first saw the room for what it was. I was too busy fighting for my life. He had me dead to rights, trapped against a stone slab with nowhere to turn, when suddenly, his eyes went wide. He stepped away and lowered his sword. 'Wait,' he said, his eyes fixed on the walls behind me. 'Look.'

"Well, there was no way I was going to turn my back on a goblin hunter. He knew that. Without a word, he circled around me so *his* back was to the wall, so I could

216

keep an eye on him while I looked at whatever he wanted me to see.

"At first, I had no idea what he was talking about. All I saw was a vine-covered wall behind a bunch of scraggly trees. But then I saw behind the trees and under the vines, images carved into the stone walls: A mighty tree, clearly a Mother Tree, elves *and* goblins dancing together. And there, like we all just witnessed, was a line of specters, both elves and goblins, lining up to enter a gate in the Mother Tree. The tip of my sword dipped. What was I looking at?"

"Torrin must have been thinking the same thing. 'What is this place?' he asked.

"I shook my head. 'I don't know.'

"'How can you not know? This is on elven land.'

"What could I say? I knew every valley, every tree, every stone in my territory. How could I have never seen this before? 'I... I just don't. It's never been here. I don't understand.'

"Then, there was a buzzing, just like we all heard today, coming from a stone altar under the carved Mother Tree. There was a sword, half-buried in the stone." Alistar pointed at Torrin's sword, still in Na'lah's hand. "That sword."

Na'lah turned her father's sword over in her hands. "Papa's sword?"

Alistar shook his head. "That was never Torrin's sword."

"But Papa said he got it from his father."

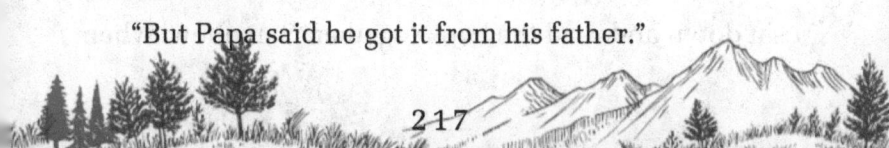

Alistar offered a slight smile. "Maybe he stretched the truth."

Na'lah's gut clenched. "Stretched the truth?"

Alistar held up a hand. "Let me finish."

Garak growled and studied the forest behind them. "Hurry up. I don't want to get caught out in the open."

Alistar smiled. "I'd expect nothing less from Torrin's son. Patience, Garak. I'm almost done."

Garak shook his head and waved for Alistar to continue.

"We went to the altar, the sword glowing and buzzing more and more with every step. Just as we got to the altar, Torrin grabbed the sword and pulled the blasted thing right out of the stone! I was about to curse him out, but as soon as the sword was free, the altar top split in half and there, in an opening, was a book."

Na'lah perked up. "The book you showed me in your tent!"

Hobler's face twisted in confusion. "What book?"

Na'lah sputtered, trying to get the words out fast enough. "It's a book, maybe magic or something. Basically, it says that elves and goblins used to be allies. Something about how we had to work together to take care of the Mother Trees and guide spirits of the deceased from the Gray Mists or the In-Between or whatever you want to call it into the Halls of the Dead." She looked at Alistar. "Did I get that right?"

Alistar shrugged. "Good enough for now. Torrin and I sat down and read the book together. Somehow, when

I looked at the book, I saw an Elvish script. When Torrin read it, the script was in Goblin. Magic! But together, that's when we learned the truth about the Mother Trees, the truth about needing to work as one. We started putting things together. Why would the Elders of both our people be lying to us? Why were the priests and Shamankas deceiving their flocks? The answer was obvious: Greed and power.

"We understood what we had in our hands. If anyone from either of the councils knew what we had found, our lives would be forfeit. Just then, we heard a baby crying from the foot of the carved Mother Tree."

Na'lah stiffened. "A baby?"

"Not just any baby," Alistar smiled. "You."

A wave passed through Na'lah. She swayed back and forth. Garak and Hobler steadied her. "You okay?" Hobler asked.

Na'lah shook her head. "What? No. Papa and Mother are my parents."

Alistar sighed. "They raised you, yes. But you are not their natural child."

"But why did Papa take me? Why not you?"

Alistar shrugged. "That was Torrin's idea. When we found you, we didn't know what you were. Not exactly an elf. Not exactly a goblin. In the end, we decided you looked more like a goblin than an elf, despite the ears. And the blue eyes." He cleared his throat. "And the pale skin."

Na'lah touched her forehead, her mind spinning. Images of herself as a youngling, sitting on Papa's lap as they watched the sun set. Lessons with Mother at the Mother Tree temple in Draal, learning the intricacies of ritual dances that were passed from mother to daughter, dances that would open the gateway to the Halls of the Dead. Dances that fell on deaf ears. Or did they? "I don't understand," she whispered. "They *both* knew? If Mother knew, why was she always so... difficult?"

Garak snorted. "Really? You know how she is. Gods save anyone who doesn't do what she thinks is best."

"But we were always fighting! Her stubbornness practically drove me away from becoming a Shamanka."

"Stubborn?" Garak smirked. "Like mother, like daughter."

Na'lah sighed. "Point taken. But why did they have to lie to me?"

Alistar considered. "Why did they lie? Sometimes, you must lie to keep a greater truth alive."

Na'lah's stomach clenched. "What are you talking about? A lie is a lie. They lied about being my parents. They lied about the Mother Tree in Draal being alive. They lied about the dances. All of it, lies!"

Alistar held up his hands. "Na'lah, Torrin couldn't tell you the truth."

"Why not?"

"Your life depended on it. If he had told you when you were younger, you might have let the secret slip. You know how children can be. And if the wrong person found out... everything would be ruined. The secret of the Mother Tree would expose the corruption inside both Councils. They would kill your parents and you to keep that secret hidden."

"But if they knew the truth, if the people knew the truth, we could end the war between goblins and elves!"

A grim smile formed on Alistar's lips. "People in power never give it up willingly."

Na'lah clenched Papa's sword, her sword. "Maybe," she said. "But now we know the truth. We can change things."

Elisara snorted. "How are we going to do that?"

Na'lah looked at the gathered elves and goblins. "Alistar, you've got a good connection with the common people, right?"

"Yes."

"And your personal guard? They know this as well?"

"Some, but not all."

"What if I visited the surrounding villages with you? I can try to awaken the local Mother Trees. Let the people see their deceased passing into the Halls of the Dead. If people saw what we saw today, do you think they could be convinced?"

Alistar considered. "Maybe. But it would be dangerous. Once word of your existence gets out, the Elven Council will seek to assassinate you at every turn."

Na'lah smirked and put a hand on Garak and Hobler's shoulders. "I'm not worried. I have these two lunks and Skronk keeping an eye on me."

Klier pressed close. "Hey! Don't forget about me!"

Na'lah frowned. "You? You keep appearing and disappearing at all the wrong times. How can I trust you?"

Klier bit his lip. "It's complicated."

Garak growled. "Blazing Sky Fire, we don't have time for this." He turned to Na'lah. "When we visited Mother and the old man after I got out of the Iron Box, he told me Klier was working as a messenger between him and Alistar."

Elisandra looked at Klier and snorted. "You were working for Alistar this whole time? What were we paying you for?"

Na'lah stiffened. "What? Klier was working for you too?"

"How do you think we got into Draal so easily?"

Na'lah scowled at Klier. "You cost me two fingers."

Klier shrugged. "Yeah, I didn't know they were going to go that far. Sorry about that. I was just doing what Torrin told me to do. His very words were, 'Get Na'lah to Alistar no matter the cost.'"

Na'lah shook her head. "Seems I can't trust anyone."

"Well," Elisandra said, her visage grim, "you can trust me. What I saw today changes everything." The elven captain touched her forehead and then her chest, the elven sign of reverence. She knelt before Na'lah and drew her sword, offering it hilt first to Na'lah. "By my blade, I vow to protect the Blended, Keeper of the Gate, Child of the Mother Tree."

Na'lah froze. "Why are you kneeling?" She shot Alistar a glance. "What am I supposed to do?"

"Take her sword," Alistar whispered, "and touch the tip to her shoulders."

Na'lah did as she was bid and then returned the sword to Elisara, who resheathed her weapon and stood up. Elf and goblin regarded one another. The angry look in Elisara's eyes was gone, replaced with something Na'lah had never seen, but had felt, when she touched the Mother Tree for the first time: reverence.

Na'lah's breath caught in her throat. This wasn't what she wanted. *Are they mistaking me for the magic? I'm nothing! Just a tool!* Despite her misgivings, she wanted to say something, to acknowledge the change that had overcome Elisandra, but before she could find her tongue, the gathered elven rangers and soldiers followed Elisara's lead. They touched their foreheads and then their chests. Na'lah looked to Alistar. "Why... why are they doing that?"

"Why? Are you serious? Look what you just did. You are the Blade, the Book, and the Blended. You awakened the Mother Tree! You are the trinity elvenkind has been waiting for."

"What?" Na'lah gasped. "Me? No! I'm just me! I'm no one!"

Alistar smiled. "Not anymore, Blended."

As one, the gathered elves knelt and held their drawn swords before Na'lah. "By our blades, for the Blended!"

Alistar grunted. "Well, it looks like you won't be alone."

Na'lah of the Short Bow, Ghost Girl of Draal, swallowed against the tightness of her throat. "I guess not." One by one, she took the hilts of the offered swords and accepted their vows of protection.

When she was done, she stood before them, flanked by her brother and partner. The elves' eyes, heavy upon her, made Na'lah squirm in her skin. She gripped Papa's sword and drew strength from the tingling in the hilt. She took a breath and gave Alistar a nod. "Are you ready?"

Alistar smiled. "More than you can know."

"Three hunters and a unit of elven rangers and soldiers," Garak said, nodding at Na'lah. "Will that be enough?"

Na'lah nodded. "It should. Wait. Three hunters? Klier, Skronk, Hobler, and you make four."

"Not me, Ghost Girl. I'm heading back to Draal."

"Draal? Why?"

"There are some things I need to take care of."

"Like what?"

"Like Mother."

Na'lah's chest tightened. Losing Papa, and now Badwin? "She's not going to take this well."

Garak shrugged. "She might take it better than you think, once she knows the whole story."

"She'll never believe me."

"Of course not," Garak said, adjusting the straps of his adventure pack. "But she'll believe me."

"What are you saying?"

"Leave Mother to me. I'll fill her in. You focus on helping the elves for now. Give me a month to have her cool down, and then you four," he said, gesturing to Na'lah, Skronk, Hobler, and Klier, "meet me at the Mother Tree temple in Draal. I'll get things ready."

"What are you going to do?"

"Me?" Garak smirked. "I'll be laying the groundwork for your triumphant return."

And so began the most surreal month of Na'lah's life. She, one of Draal's elite hunters, was traveling from elven village to village in the company of elven rangers as she reawakened their Mother Trees, called the spirits of deceased elves to pass into the Halls of the Dead, and converted former elven enemies to, *What even was this?*, a new movement for peace and reconciliation. With Alistar and Elisara's help, along with the converts from the elven rangers who had witnessed Na'lah's initial works in Ahman'Dur, Na'lah spread the message of unity from valley to valley.

After three weeks, their small party had grown to hundreds. The collection of elves accompanied them from village to village. Even Askabar, the small elven village where all of this started, found its small Mother Tree revitalized and its populace clamoring for peace with their long-time foes.

There were those who protested, of course, but what argument could stand in the face of seeing the dead finally admitted to their well-deserved rest in the Halls of the Dead? Even the assassination attempts became fewer and fewer as the strength of the movement grew. Mother's words from years before echoed daily in Na'lah's heart.

Mother was right.

This is who Na'lah was meant to be. This is what she was meant to do.

After three weeks, though, it was time for Na'lah to return to Draal. That was what she had promised Garak, anyway. And, as much as she was coming to appreciate these former enemies of hers, Na'lah knew she couldn't put off facing her mother any longer.

She gathered the elves together, and, with Alistar and Elisara at her side, turned the task of preparing the elves of Acorium, the elven capital, over to the elves themselves. "I'll be back," she promised. "But first, I need to visit Draal."

And so, with a stout regiment of elven rangers led by Elisara herself, Na'lah and her fellow hunters made their way to the border between their lands. Elisara stood with Na'lah on the banks of the Bear Hill River, at a site known as the Bloody Fords. The elven ranger put her hands on Na'lah's shoulders. "You should let us come with you," Elisara insisted. "I don't feel safe letting you travel alone."

Na'lah laughed. "I'm not alone," she said, looking at Hobler, Skronk, and Klier, who were negotiating fares with a bargeman who stared with wide eyes at the party of elven rangers. "They might not be the brightest, but they're good in a pinch. And don't forget, I was a hunter before I was a Shamanka."

Elisara frowned and glanced at Na'lah's missing fingers. "A hunter without her shooting fingers." She paused. "I'm sorry about that."

Na'lah held up her mangled hand. "It's alright. I'm not sure I need them anymore. Arrows aren't the only way to get rid of an enemy."

Elisara smiled, and then bowed, touching her forehead and her chest. "As you say, Blended." Then she turned, and without another word, melted into the forested mountainside with the rest of the rangers.

Na'lah watched them leave and took a slow, calming breath. As terrifying as facing the truth of her past had been, a part of her was even more afraid of facing Mother. How was she going to react to hearing that Badwin was gone? How would she react to learning that Na'lah had grown into whatever this was? And what would she say now that the truth of Na'lah's past was known? So many questions.

Hobler crunched through the river-rounded pebbles from the barge, shaking his head the whole way. "A silver for each of us! Can you believe it? There was a time when being a hunter meant something."

Na'lah chuckled. "Maybe it will mean something different from now on."

Hobler nodded. "Maybe." He cleared his throat and looked back at Klier and Skronk, who were loading their light packs onto the barge. Hesitantly, he took Na'lah's hands in his. "Hey, you okay?"

"Yeah. I think so."

Hobler studied her face. "You sure?"

"Yeah... no. I just don't know how Mother is going to be when I see her."

"Well, no sense in getting worked up about it now. You can't control that."

"I know. But you know how she is."

"I do." Hobler looked over his shoulder again at Klier and Skronk, who were talking to the bargeman now. Seeing they were distracted, he pulled Na'lah into an embrace.

Na'lah shook her head. "Still being secretive, are we?"

Hobler sighed. "Maybe. I don't want to be, but you know. Garak and all."

Na'lah pushed away. "I thought we worked through this already."

"I did too. I–" and then he stopped and closed his eyes. "You know what? You're right. You've always been right. When we get back to Draal, we'll talk to Garak, alright? Together."

Na'lah smirked. "About time."

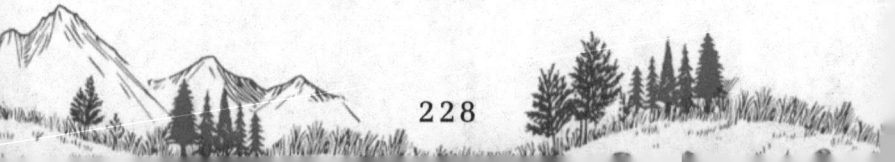

Then, taking Hobler's hand, Na'lah led Hobler across the stony beach to the barge, where Klier and Skronk were waiting for them. Who, Na'lah noted with a smile, didn't even bat an eye at seeing them holding hands.

19

The Ending of a Start, Or Start Of An Ending? I Get Confused.

week later, Na'lah found her mother and brother in Draal at the Temple near the Mother Tree, arguing amongst the members of the Council of Elders. Master Goggins, leaning on his cane with a blank face, was a pace behind Garak, but not involved in the heated discussion. He seemed focused on what they were doing to Garak.

Soldiers held Garak's arms behind his back, restraining him while he shouted. Na'lah could not hear what they were saying, but by the way her mother was flailing her hands, she knew it was not good. As she got closer, she heard snippets of her brother's shouts. "Elven Grove... restored... listen... Na'lah... opened the path...

not enemies." The shouting was drawing a crowd. A small group of soldiers rushed to hold people back.

Na'lah spotted Elder Narlak. His face was strewn with anger. Spittle dripped down his chin. "You," he said, raising a finger and pointing right at Na'lah as she approached. "You are a traitor to your people. You are hereby stripped of your honors as a hunter. Guards! Arrest her! Take her to the Iron Box where she will rot for the rest of her days!" Some of the soldiers keeping the crowd back encircled Na'lah, swords drawn.

"And slay that one where he stands," Narlak snarled, pointing now at Garak. "He escaped from the Iron Box once, but he can't escape death."

"That isn't your call, Elder Narlak," Master Goggins said, taking a small step forward.

"Don't forget your place, Master Goggins. You only train hunters. The Council uses them for our purposes," Narlak spat out.

"The Council's purposes, yes, but for one man's vengeance, no," Master Goggins replied. "It seems I will have to revamp my training to include an awareness of one's actions."

"I can have you replaced as well, Goggins, if you continue!" Narlak retorted.

Garak surged against his restraints. "Na'lah!"

Mother stood with an impassive face, her arms crossed over her chest.

The murmuring crowd pushed forward, trying to get a glimpse of the situation.

Na'lah, hearing the accusations, strode towards the Council of Elders, not bothering to glance at the guards threatening her. A tingle ran through her body. Her vision sharpened, taking in the small details of her surroundings. Eldar Narlak's clenched hand. The bead of sweat running down his face. The other members of the Council leaning subtly away from Narlak after his outburst. Nervous glances bouncing between them.

"We have been lied to!" she shouted as she spun around, announcing to the crowd who watched her with expectant expressions. "A Council member here has sought war with the elves all along!"

The crowd mumbled. From the back came a shout. "What of it? We hate the elves!"

"That has not always been the way," Na'lah called. "This war between the races began with greed. And it continues to grow because of greed. The Mother Tree went dormant because of that greed. We lost our way in the Spirit World because of greed, and it left our dead to wander in the Gray Mist. That greed stripped our Shamankas of their power to release those spirits to the Halls of the Dead. I know. I have seen it."

The murmuring became louder. Snippets of "Ghost Girl" and "blue eyes" punctuated the murmuring, but also, "so many missions successful" and "respected hunter."

She continued. "We goblins, and even the elves, have been laying down our lives to fight for the benefit of a few. To make their purses heavier at the cost of our dead.

I know. I am Na'lah of the Short Bow. But I am the guiltiest of you all. I helped fatten those purses by following the orders from *him*." Na'lah pointed right at Narlak. "I closed my mind to the possibility that there is another way for our people. But no more! There *is* another path. A path that not only connects us as goblins, but a path that connects goblins to elves to resurrect the magic of the Mother Tree."

A voice rang out from the crowd. "The Council members and Shamankas say the spirits are passing through the Gray Mist because of our sacrifices to the Mother Tree. We do not need the elves for that."

"But we do!" came a voice from behind the crowd.

Na'lah turned and saw the crowd part as Hobler, Skronk, and Klier walked forward.

"We bear witness to what Na'lah has said," Hobler continued. "The Mother Tree has never asked for coin in the past! It needed peace on both sides to reawaken, and Na'lah gave us that. We saw her open the gates and allow spirits to pass, both goblins and elves. The Council of Elders has stripped our history from us!"

Narlak pushed past the other Council members. "Enough of this nonsense! Guards! Arrest her! Arrest all of them! And if they resist, kill them." He was shaking, panic in his eyes.

One of the Council members leaned towards Narlak. "You assured us you had this under control."

"I do, you fool," Narlak spat. "Master Goggins, go and retrieve some of your hunters to control this rebel group you created!"

Master Giggins spread his arms wide. "I did not create eyes that are now open, Elder Narlak. I created hunters who protect Draal."

"Heresy. Traitor! Guards, kill them! Kill them all!" Narlak shouted.

"You must listen to her!" Hobler cried. "The Mother Tree brings us together!"

The soldiers holding the crowd back advanced toward the small group, swords out.

Then everything happened at once. Hobler barreled through the circle of guards surrounding Na'lah, sending two of them flying. Klier and Skronk charged in, right on his heels. They took positions around Na'lah with swords drawn. Hobler bent his bow.

Na'lah held up her hands. "I will deal with this."

With that, the three fell a step behind her. This was her fight. She unsheathed Papa's blade and held it before her. It glowed and hummed throughout Na'lah's body.

"See? She has an elven blade! She is a traitor to our kind!" Narlak screamed. "She is not one of us. She is the Ghost Girl!"

Seeing the elven blade, soldiers sprang to life. Na'lah's group was outnumbered four to one, but they were better trained. Metal clashed as the two small groups collided. Skronk and Klier's blades swirled in the air, defending against the onslaught. Hobler loosed arrow after arrow at the soldiers, wounding many. When a soldier got too close, he used his bow as a club to send them flying.

Na'lah parried two attacks with her sword, catching the first one over her shoulder then swinging forward to thwart the thrust of the second. She spun on her heels and kicked the first attacker square in the gut, sending him to the ground. She leapt to the side before his body stopped rolling. The second attacker lunged again. Na'lah twisted away and caught his sword arm tugging slightly up and then brought it straight down. The momentum caused the soldier to flip in midair and land on his back.

Skronk and Klier engaged the soldiers on Hobler's sides. Skronk had short blades in each hand. He whirled like a tornado, ducking attacks and countering with slashes to mid-sections when he got in close. Klier's blade spun in the air and came sweeping down upon soldiers, knocking them back. But when one soldier was knocked aside, two more filled the spot.

"There are too many, Na'lah! And we do not want to kill our own kind!" Hobler swung his bow, connecting with the side of a soldier's head. "We need to get out of here, or we are all going to die."

Na'lah paused. Not far from her, Garak's captor crumpled to the ground with an arrow through each leg. She scanned the clearing and saw Master Goggins a few paces away nocking another arrow. Na'lah nodded her thanks to the old weapon's master.

"Garak, clear us a path!" Na'lah commanded.

He nodded and started for the outer ring of soldiers. Hope glimmered until a hand snaked out to stop him. *Mother.*

"You were wrong, Garak. Look what she has done here. She has chosen to be a hunter."

"She is the Blended, Mother. You must trust me."

Na'lah watched the exchange before ducking under another sword. It just missed her head. She turned and punched up, knocking the wind out of her attacker. As he doubled over, another arrow knocked her attacker to the ground, an arrow through the shoulder. *Master Goggins' work.*

She turned. "Klier, Skronk, Hobler, advance towards Garak. We have to get out of here! I am right behind you!"

Hobler grunted and swung his bow, taking the legs from beneath a soldier. "Got it, Na'lah. But we are not leaving without you!"

Na'lah turned and advanced to where the three were holding off the guards. She slipped through the fighting, exchanging positions with them in the blink of an eye. Na'lah's back was now to the Council, facing the soldiers and the crowd. She just hoped that Garak could make a path for them to find some breathing room. They had to regroup. This was all going really bad, really quick.

The circle surrounding them tightened like a noose. Na'lah shot a quick glance over her shoulder and saw the three still fighting but becoming sluggish from the effort. *They just keep coming. And we can't deliver a killing blow... that would defeat our purpose here*, Na'lah felt herself draining from the effort.

"Garak, if you are going to do something, do it now!" Na'lah screamed.

She blocked a swipe meant to relieve her head from her body and found herself stumbling into Hobler's legs. She dropped her sword, trying to find her footing. She flailed her arms and caught the back of Hobler's tunic. A blade zipped in, straight for her throat.

"Grip!" Hobler screamed, and in one swift moment, the big man spun.

Na'lah tightened her grip on the back of his tunic. The motion propelled Na'lah into the air, lifting and spinning her around. Her boot caught the guard's head just as the blade was about to impale her. The guard was knocked off his feet, and his sword clattered to the ground. When Na'lah made a full revolution, she let go and rolled to the side, grabbing her sword and came to a three-point stance, sword in hand. She looked at the guard and found another arrow protruding from his arm. *That's three I owe you, Master.*

Na'lah stood. "Garak!"

At that moment, a roar and a staccato of metal on metal echoed near the temple. Na'lah turned to see a blur of gray, Garak, cutting through the outer circle of the guards near the Council members and Mother. And in that moment, a gap formed in the line.

"Go!" Na'lah fully turned towards the opening.

Hobler, Skronk, and Klier took off with Na'lah a step behind them. They passed the ring of soldiers and guards at a dead run, sprinted past the Council members, and even past Mother. The Shamanka Temple was to their right, behind the Council. The dormant Mother Tree lay directly before them. If they made it past the Mother Tree, maybe they could escape to the forest beyond.

"Get to the woods!" Na'lah screamed, still trailing the three in front. She glanced back to see if Garak and Master Goggins were following.

"Garak, Master, move! We need to leave!"

Garak turned from the fight. "*You* need to move! You are the Blended, Na'lah."

"I'm not leaving you!"

"Find Alistar! Listen to him! He will help you!"

A crow squawked.

In that moment, a blade ran Garak through, full to the hilt. Narlak released the handle, and Garak fell.

Master Goggins lowered his bow and ran to Garak.

Goggins was a hair's breadth away when suddenly he stiffened and stumbled, Narlak's dagger in his side. Narlak snarled and pulled the dagger out and then plunged it in again and again.

Master Goggins fell, lifeless.

"No!" Na'lah screamed.

Trying to switch her momentum and course back to her brother, she tripped over a Mother Tree root and

sprawled forward. Her hand hit the bark of the tree, trying to gain purchase.

Energy raced through her body, and she was thrown to the ground.

A shockwave emanated outward, knocking everyone back. Na'lah, on hands and knees, shook her head. Garak and Master Goggins lay in heaps on the ground.

"Garak! Master! No!" She scrambled towards them.

Master Goggins' body lay still, but Garak's chest was shivering. She grabbed him and hugged him tight in her lap. She fought to stand with him and stumbled. Guards, soldiers, council members, villagers, and Mother stood about and stared. At first, she thought they were staring at her. *Not me,* she realized, *something behind me.* She turned to see the Mother Tree sprouting new leaves at an incredible rate. A low humming pulsed the air around it.

Glowing veins pumped life through the trunk of the tree, up and out to the branches. More leaves sprouted, fully grown and as green as the forest during the rainy season. The new canopy cast a shadow over all, blocking out the sun. Life radiated from the tree.

Just as quickly, the glowing and pulsing stopped and all that was heard was a low hum, much like at Ahman'Dur, leaving a vibrant, growing, live Mother Tree standing before them.

Na'lah turned back and saw a stunned crowd staring at the new Mother Tree. Hobler, Skronk, and Klier pushed through the crowd to stand at Na'lah's side. Hobler looked up at the growing Mother Tree and then back at Na'lah. "You did it again," he whispered.

Na'lah nodded. "But I don't know how."

A piercing scream split the crowd's silence. Mother was running right at her. She pushed Na'lah away and grabbed Garak.

Na'lah stood dumbly and watched Mother rocking her eldest son. "My boy, my boy!" Mother cried.

The shock of seeing the reviving Mother Tree gave way in the face of her own mother's grief. Na'lah clenched her fists. "No, no, no!" Na'lah cried. She whirled on the Mother Tree. "No more! Have I not given enough? What more do you want from me?"

Spirits of the deceased began to appear, goblins and elves, exactly as they did in the grove of Ahman'Dur. They surrounded Garak and then parted to make a path from the tree. The low hum grew louder, and then faded, opening a gateway. A Spirit Walker came out and moved towards Na'lah.

"You!" she shouted and pointed sharply at the figure emerging. "I did what you asked, and this is my reward? Losing all my family? If that is the case, take your sword, your book, and your prophecy. I want nothing to do with this anymore."

"You have not lost all, Na'lah. You still have your mother and others," the Spirit Walker hissed.

"Mother? She doesn't care for me or my choices. And I want nothing to do with her. She wants me out of her life, and I am happy to oblige. She was the true believer in this, not me. She is useless."

"Not to The Mist, she is not."

"Then use her, not me."

"She is useful, yes, but you are necessary."

"If I am so necessary, why are you taking everything from me?"

"To give you something back." And with that, the Spirit Walker grabbed Na'lah's wrist and tugged. Na'lah tried to pull away, but the bony fingers were like a vice. The grip was cold, lifeless. Energy connected her with the Spirit Walker. It flowed from one to the other.

"What are you doing? Stop this!" Na'lah shouted.

The Spirit Walker dragged Na'lah towards Mother and Garak. Mother looked up. "You! You get away from him. You have no right to be near my son!"

Garak was still breathing, but it was shallow.

"This is not my choice, Mother!" Na'lah shot back. "I was dragged here under protest."

"Dragged, dragged by what, you insolent girl?"

She cannot see the Spirit Walker.

"I don't care to hear your delusions," Mother continued. "You made your choice to be a hunter and destroyed my family in the process. I have nothing more to say." She turned from Na'lah and wept.

Na'lah whirled on the Spirit Walker. "See what my involvement got me? The death of my family and..."

The Spirit Walker tugged her violently towards Garak's body. "Garak was correct at the Grove of

Ahman'Dur. You do have the power to heal in you. You have many powers. You simply must reach for them." The Walker placed Na'lah's hand over the wound in Garak's side.

"Get your filthy..." Mother trailed off.

Na'lah glanced at Mother, but Mother's attention was no longer on her. Mother was looking behind Na'lah, a look of shock plastered over her face. "You... you are a Spirit Walker," Mother breathed. "But... but. Where did you come from?"

"Mother of Na'lah. Now is not the time for questions. You and I have much to discuss later. For now, Na'lah needs to concentrate on Garak."

"But, but," Mother stuttered.

"Silence. Continue, Na'lah."

A familiar tingling sensation ran throughout Na'lah's body.

"Focus."

Na'lah looked at the hand lying on Garak's wound.

"Concentrate."

She forced the sensation to collect at that point.

"Release."

She let go and felt the flow go from her into Garak. The wound wriggled, its edges coming together. The knitting came slowly at first, but the more she concentrated, the faster it worked. Garak's breathing

deepened. Finally, the wound closed. The tingling sensation faded. Garak relaxed into an easy sleep.

Na'lah looked at her hands. Maybe, just maybe, this Spirit Walker had been telling her the truth all along. She turned to Mother, who was now looking at her with amazement.

"Mother, I, I... don't understand," Na'lah stammered.

Mother reached out and touched her cheek, her eyes full of wonder as she looked upon her daughter. "How can you not understand? You are the promised one. The Blended. Torrin told me to be patient, to look deeper, to wait, but I couldn't. I only ever saw you as a..."

"Disappointment?" Na'lah answered coldly.

"No, never a disappointment," Mother said. "A stubborn, foolhardy, strong-headed girl. A girl that had so much potential at her fingertips and refused to see it. A girl who could change the world and got caught up in her own dreams. But never a disappointment."

"But all these years you chastised me?" Na'lah's brow furrowed in confusion.

"Shush, child. Let a weary mother apologize. Torrin was right all along. You had to find your own way. He was such a patient man. Your stubbornness, foolhardiness, and strong headedness you get from me. I tried to push you to find your potential, but now I see that I only succeeded in pushing you away. For that, I am truly sorry... daughter."

Na'lah felt the tension start to drain from her body. She placed her hand over her mother's. They stayed like that for a moment until shouting broke the trance.

"This changes nothing! They are still traitors to our kind!" Narlak screamed as he strode towards them, the other council members right behind him. "Kill them! Kill them all. They have brought some elven magic back to trick us into believing this is real. We must prepare for war!"

Mother shot up. "This," she gestured to the fully alive Mother Tree, "is real, Elder Narlak. Can you not feel it? It is back, and Na'lah has brought it back."

"You were exiled. Why should we believe a thing you say? This is part of a scheme to wriggle your way back into power!"

Mother stood toe-to-toe with Narlak. "Not on this, no, but on your plan to get rich by using the Shamanka for your own greed, Elder. Yes, we went along with your scheme so the Shamanka would bring peace and comfort to those who lost people, but when you choose to blackmail our faith for your greed, you went too far."

"You have no proof of this," Narlak shot back.

Na'lah stood and stepped forward, Hobler and Skronk at her sides. "The proof is in front of you, Narlak. And if that is not enough, I can share with the Council the mission you assigned to me in private, 'Off the books' you said."

Na'lah turned and saw Klier, Skronk, and Hobler standing protectively behind her, ready to defend her on her command, hands hovering over their swords.

"And I have a few more of those stories about using hunters for your gains, Narlak," Klier said. "I have been watching Na'lah and you for quite some time."

A Council member stepped forward, "Narlak, it seems we, as a council, need to talk with you about these accusations." He held up a hand to stop Narlak. "Yes, we know one is from an exile, an exile you personally signed the papers for. The other is from a well-decorated and respected hunter. That alone would put you to question. But your actions here, impaling Garak and stabbing Master Goggins repeatedly right after what seems to be new life for the Mother Tree, have us questioning your loyalty and motives. Guards, arrest him... for now." The Council member turned to Na'lah and her mother. "In light of actions here, you," he pointed to Na'lah, "and your group will not be put under guard. But you are not to leave Draal until this matter is resolved. Is that clear?"

Na'lah and her mother nodded in agreement. Na'lah watched guards drag Narlak away from the scene, kicking and screaming about "traitors to our kind." She finally turned to her lifeless master, sorrow hitting her in the chest. She knelt, silent sobs raking through her body as she closed his eyes. "I will miss you, Master. You were always there for me. You were the light that..."

Garak coughed and tried to sit up. Na'lah and Mother clutched at the blood-soaked hunter, but he brushed their hands aside. "Enough. Blazing Sky Fire. You're going to tear me apart."

Mother ignored his request and hugged her eldest son tighter. "I thought you were dead."

"I was. Almost."

Mother's mouth flapped. "What?"

Garak lifted his chin at Na'lah. "I was passing through The Mist, and this one pulled me back. Hmm... I guess the old man was right."

Na'lah scrunched up her face. "What?"

"It wasn't *my* choice. You think I like answering your questions twice?"

Na'lah looked at her hands. "I thought I just healed you."

"Wow. Ears that big and you still can't hear?"

Na'lah looked at her sword. She picked it up off the ground where she dropped it to get to Garak. She held the hilt and turned the blade slowly back and forth. "Maybe Alistar was right. I am The Blended. The only one."

Garak snorted. "Hey, *warrok*, don't get too cocky. I was just in The Mist, and I saw *one* thing very clearly. You are not the only one who can do what you just did."

"I'm not?"

"No. There are others, and they are coming for you."

"What?"

"Yup, so do yourself a favor before that happens and grab Hobler."

"Hobler? Why?"

Garak snorted. "Three years in the Iron Box didn't make me blind, and I'm sick of pretending I don't know about you two."

Na'lah and Hobler exchanged looks. Hobler's face flushed. "You knew?"

Garak snorted and tried to stand but fell back on his seat. "Everyone knew. And everyone approved. Not like that matters, but they did."

Na'lah looked at Klier and Skronk, who just smirked and shrugged. Hobler blinked. "I thought you would be mad."

Garak shook his head. "Why the blazes would anyone care what I thought?"

"But," Hobler started.

"But nothing," Garak interrupted. He held his hands up. "Now, someone help me up. It's been three years since I've had an ale, and there's no one I'd rather hoist one with than my amazing, stubborn, *warrok* of a sister."

Na'lah grabbed Garak's hand and pulled him to his feet. "First round's on me," she said, and pulled him into a hug.

Acknowledgements:

No book is ever written alone, and Finish the Mission is no exception. The authors would like to acknowledge the contributions of the following people in the creation of this book:

- ☐ To Kim Suhr, for your excellent insight and feedback. You are the best writing teacher we could ever ask for. Anyone who has the courage to improve their craft should seek you out at Red Oak Writing.

- ☐ To Michael Braun, at Ten16 Press, for taking a chance on our first draft. Thank you for seeing the diamond in the rough.

- ☐ To Nahla Kansier and Khloe Weidensee, for being artist models for our first drawings...and also unintentionally inspiring a great name for a goblin hunter!

- ☐ To Christopher Keefe, for your eternal patience when this book's artist interrupted your days demanding feedback and drawing advice. Also, thank you for your valuable feedback on our early drafts. You are an excellent teacher, an amazing artist, and a good friend.

☐ To Scott Curty, for your early read of the second draft AND the professional photography of the artwork. Your generosity knows no bounds, and Michael doubts he will ever harvest enough honey to pay you back for your kindness.

☐ To our adult beta readers, Anna Baxter-Bauer, Thomas Baxter, William Ringelstetter, Kevin Strattan, Marieke Gilmartin, Michelle Syverson-Weber, Hunter Weber, the Schlueter family, and the Klein family. Your experience with the fantasy genre, story structure, and honest feedback made this a better story.

☐ To our student beta readers, Ian Daubert, Omarian Dennis, and Gloria Bartelt. Thank you for feedback from our target audience. Your insight into the minds of young readers was invaluable!

☐ To our wives, for the hours away from home as we huddled over a table at the Broken Axe in Draal, drafting and redrafting Na'lah's story. Thank you for believing in us...and your patience!

Michael Weber teaches high school history, creative writing, and film in Wales, Wisconsin. An ardent believer in the power of storytelling, Michael emphasizes the importance of students becoming the protagonists of their own tales. When not writing fiction or drawing accompanying artwork, Michael is busy being a husband, dad, beekeeper, and chicken wrangler. Visit Michael on his Instagram page @mr.weberdoesstuff.

Brian Zeiler teaches high school English, guided reading, creative writing, and science fiction in Wales, Wisconsin. A voracious reader of YA, Brian believes that if you say you do not like to read, you just haven't found your niche. When not getting bullied by Mike to write, Brian is running around after his two boys: Beck and Dax, and doing whatever his wife Kari says. Visit Brian on his Instagram page @MrZeilerreads.

Also by Michael Weber,
The New Apprentice

Derek Fulstarter fancies himself a hero, but his quick temper keeps him in hot water. Like this morning, when a street fight with the neighborhood bully, Conrad, got him arrested, landing both of them in the stockades on Ploughman's Wharf. When they witness the bully's sister, Dani, getting kidnapped, Derek has to make a choice—be the hero he imagines himself to be or let the bully figure things out on his own.

With a little push from a mentor, Derek realizes it's time to put up or shut up. He and Conrad escape the stockade and set off on an adventure with swaggering swordsmen, towering minotaurs, and pirates on the high seas to save the kidnapped children. Along the way, Derek discovers a new friend in Conrad, as well as admiration for Dani, who proves to be much stronger than Derek realized.